THE LAST WICKED SCOUNDREL

Also by Lorraine Heath

Fiction

THE LAST WICKED SCOUNDREL

A Scoundrels of St. James Novella

LORRAINE HEATH

AVONIMPULSE
An Imprint of HarperCollinsPublishers

Excerpt from *When the Duke Was Wicked* copyright © 2014 by Jan Nowasky.

Excerpt from *Santa, Bring My Baby Back* copyright © 2013 by Cheryl Harper.

Excerpt from *The Christmas Cookie Chronicles: Grace* copyright © 2013 by Laurie Vanzura.

Excerpt from *Desperately Seeking Fireman* copyright © 2014 by Jennifer Bernard.

EPub Edition JANUARY 2014 ISBN: 9780062317155

Print Edition ISBN: 9780062317162

JV 10 9 8

*For all my lovely readers who give my characters
a home in their hearts.*

PROLOGUE

From the Journal of William Graves

I was born to a woman who deemed me worthless, except when I provided her with a convenient spot for the back of her hand. I learned well to avoid her, to hide in corners, to find a way to be far from her reach. As soon as my legs could keep up, I began to accompany my father on his nightly runs to the graveyards.

He was a grave robber, you see. And he treated me much more kindly than did my mum. He saw potential in me, because I was willing to help him dig for the treasures. That was what he called them. Often the well-to-do were buried with their jewelry. Some fancy gents had gold teeth. All were cadavers, needed by the hospital for teaching potential physicians about the intricacies of the human body, and they put coins in my father's pockets.

I never feared the dead. They could no longer hurt me.

When my mum died, my father took her straightaway to the hospital because she would fetch us a tidy sum. But that time—after they paid my father—I lingered about, caught glimpses of the reverence with which the bodies were handled and the secrets they revealed.

When I returned home, my father was gone. I never saw him

again. I don't know if he was robbed and killed for his flush pockets or if he decided he wanted to be rid of me, realized my mum was correct and I wasn't worth the effort of keeping alive.

I was eight at the time, and soon found myself on the streets where I fell in with a fellow who went by the name of Feagan. He managed a group of child thieves, and soon taught me to rob swells of their silk handkerchiefs. My fingers were nimble and quick, well suited to the task.

However, Fate is a fickle lady. Eventually it was discovered that one of Feagan's lads was actually a lost child of the aristocracy, and when Luke went to live with his grandfather, the Earl of Claybourne, he took me with him. I was tutored in mathematics, penmanship, and reading. When I was of a proper age, I gained admittance to a teaching hospital.

I was comfortable around the cadavers, eager to understand all they could share with me. In time, I was able to apply what I learned. I became a renowned physician, treating the poor and aristocracy alike. Eventually, my skills became known to the queen, and she bade me to serve at her pleasure, which I did gladly.

But I never forgot my humble beginnings, never forgot that the dead always tell their secrets.

CHAPTER ONE

London
1854

Winifred Buckland, the Duchess of Avendale, had never been more terrified in her life. Something was wrong, dreadfully wrong, and she feared that if she told anyone what was happening that they would see her straightaway to Bedlam.

So as people arrived for her charity ball, she stood at the foot of the stairs that led into the grand salon and pretended nothing was amiss. With a warm smile, she thanked the most influential and affluent members of the aristocracy for coming in support of her plans to build a hospital. It was a grand undertaking, but managing the project had served to bolster her confidence.

She began hosting the event shortly after her first year of mourning. Her husband had died in a fire at Heatherwood, the Earl of Claybourne's ancestral estate. The reason for his being in the manor was still a bit murky, but his death was clear. She'd seen his charred remains and had the ducal rings removed from the ash of his fingers. With his demise had come her freedom—her freedom from pain, humiliation, and paralyzing fear. He'd been a brute, if she were honest. Although only a handful of people knew that truth. It wasn't something about which one boasted.

After greeting the latest arrivals, she experienced a small respite and took a moment to glance around. The orchestra situated in the balcony was playing a waltz. Morning lilies, her favorite flower, were arranged in lovely vases, bringing their sweet fragrance into the ballroom. Through a nearby door, her guests wandered into another room where they were greeted with an abundance of food and drink on long linen-covered tables. Champagne flowed. Laughter floated through the rooms. She loved the laughter most of all. Such a joyous sound when there had been little enough in her life for some years.

Where once arranging balls had been a tedious ordeal that often undermined her self-esteem because her husband always found fault with one thing or another, now she enjoyed the task immensely because her ball served the purpose of repaying the man who had quite literally rescued her from death's door.

Glancing back up the stairs, she felt her heart give a little stutter as she watched William Graves descending. With his blond hair curling about his head like a halo, he reminded her of an angel. Her angel. He had not only seen to her injuries, but had provided her with sanctuary after the last horrible beating her husband had given her before his accidental death.

It was because of William Graves that she hosted this affair every year. She very much intended to use the funds to establish a hospital in his honor as a way to repay him for all he'd done for her.

Finally he reached her, took her gloved hand, and pressed a kiss to it. "Your Grace, you're looking lovely this evening."

"Dr. Graves, I'm so pleased you could join us." She wished she didn't sound so breathless, as though she were the one who had just descended the stairs, and descended them at a hurried clip. She didn't know why he always made her struggle for breath, in a rather pleasant way that implied anticipation rather than dread. Considering the treatment she'd endured at the hands of her husband, she was very much surprised that she didn't fear all men.

But there was something about William Graves that had always put her at ease. The devilment dancing in the blue of his eyes perhaps or the way he smiled somewhat roguishly as though he were very adept at holding a lady's secrets, especially if he were the reason for those secrets. His was the face of Adonis, and while his evening clothes provided him with an elegance and veneer of civility, she knew power resided beneath the fabric. He had carried her with such ease three years ago. Barely conscious at the time, she'd still been extremely aware of being cocooned within the shelter of his strong arms. His voice had issued quiet but insistent commands, urging her not to succumb to death's clutches. She suspected most of his patients healed because of his unwavering insistence that they not do otherwise.

He took in his surroundings with the attention of someone who never failed to overlook the tiniest of details. "You have a rather nice turnout. I'm not sure I'd have been missed."

Rubbing the bridge of her nose, she said, "You would have been, I assure you. And you're correct about the attendance this evening. This year's donations will provide the funds to see that the work on the hospital begins in earnest."

His blue gaze came back to bear on her. "A hospital will be much appreciated. You're very generous to give it your time and such devotion."

"It's no sacrifice, I assure you. Perhaps if you have a couple of spare hours in the next few days, we could discuss some of the details. I want to ensure that it suits your needs."

"I trust your judgment."

He would never know how much those words meant to her. Her husband had sought to control every aspect of her life, had never trusted her judgment. In the end, she began to doubt it as well. "Still, I value your opinion."

"Your Grace, it should have nothing to do with me."

It had everything to do with him. "Please," she urged, knowing that next he would tell her again that he had done nothing out of the ordinary in caring for her. She liked him, rather a lot, but he kept a respectful distance and was always so formal with her. She knew he had grown up on the streets and was a friend to the Earl of Claybourne. It was how she had met him as the earl had also assisted that awful night. "It gives my life purpose. I'm going to build a hospital whether or not you assist me, but doing it on my own, I may muck things up."

He smiled, a soft upturn of his lips. "I doubt you will muck things up, but I suppose I could add some insight regarding the needs of a hospital. I'll make time in my schedule to look over your plans."

"I appreciate it."

"Now, can you make time in your hostess schedule to dance with me?"

Joy burst through her. It was the first ball where she had not worn her mourning garb. In her pale blue evening gown, she felt young again, not weighted down with the poor decisions of her youth. "I can indeed. My dance card is completely open. Widows are not nearly as sought after as young single ladies."

"Personally, I prefer a lady with some experience in life to the ones who are too innocent." The strains of another waltz started up. "Will this dance suffice?"

She couldn't contain her pleasure. "It will do very nicely."

As he led her onto the dance floor, she did experience a moment of disappointment. She would have felt far more self-possessed if she were wearing the sapphire necklace that once belonged to her mother. It would have gone perfectly with her gown and would have served to distract from her misshapen nose that listed slightly to one side—a parting gift from Avendale. But when she'd gone to the safe earlier to retrieve the sapphires, they hadn't been there. She didn't know how the necklace could have been stolen when the safe was secure and she was the only one with the key. She tried to remember when she had last worn it, and if she might have placed it elsewhere, but she always took such care with the jewelry, more because of its sentimental value than its monetary worth.

But thoughts of the necklace slipped from her mind as William Graves took her into his arms and swept her over the gleaming marble floor. Her favorite part of the evening was always this singular dance with him. He would only ask her once. It mattered not that no one else escorted her onto the dance area. After these few minutes, he wouldn't intrude on her evening again—as though she would consider any time spent with him an intrusion.

As his eyes held hers, she wondered if he saw her as she was now or as she'd been. She didn't wish to be vain, but it seemed that she was nonetheless. A diagonal white line marred one brow. She had a tiny scar on one cheek. Beneath her gown resided several others. William knew of their existence because he'd been the one to stitch her up, the one who had held ice against all the various areas that had swollen and bruised. He was the one who had spooned broth into her mouth when she could barely move her jaw.

She had been a married woman who, within only a few days, began to hold affection for a man who wasn't her husband. Then Avendale was gone, and her guilt over her feelings toward William had spiked. Entirely inappropriate for her to think of him as anything other than her physician. And William, bless him, had never taken advantage of the situation, had never indicated that he saw her as anything other than a patient.

But now she almost believed she saw desire smoldering in his eyes. They didn't speak. It seemed there was no need for words. But she was acutely aware of his hand holding hers tightly, his other hand pressing into the small of her back, his legs brushing against her skirt. He was tall, broad-shouldered, but she wasn't threatened by his physical traits. Rather, she felt safe, protected.

Perhaps it was a result of the days she'd spent under his care. He had secreted her and her son away to his town home. His friend, Frannie, who later became the Duchess of Greystone, had seen to caring for Whit, while William had devoted all his time ensuring that Winnie recovered from the ordeal. It was more than the physical healing that had been required, and he saw to her emotional needs masterfully.

So many nights she awoke with a start from a nightmare to see him sitting in a chair beside the bed keeping watch over her. He filled her hours of recovery by reading Shakespeare and Dickens to her, playing chess, carrying her out to the garden so she could enjoy watching her son kicking a ball around with Frannie. He seemed to know what she needed without her voicing it. He was so attentive, and while she told herself that it was only because he was seeing to her recovery, in a small corner of her heart she could not help but believe that he enjoyed his time with her, that he welcomed excuses to be in her company a bit longer. Sometimes they would talk about nothing in particular into the late hours of the night, until she drifted off into restful slumber. She always seemed to sleep better when she carried his voice into her dreams.

Now the music drifted into silence, and very slowly their movements came to a halt. He appeared on the verge of saying something, asking for another dance perhaps. Or at least she hoped those were the words he would utter. She didn't care if only two dances was proper. She would dance every one with him if he but asked.

Instead, he gave her a small smile and began to lead her toward the sweeping staircase where she could be on hand to greet any latecomers. Once they reached their destination, he again took her hand and kissed the back of it.

"Thank you for the dance," he said.

"It was my pleasure."

His eyes darkened. "No, Duchess, as always it was mine."

With those parting words, he strode away, becoming lost in the thicket of guests. She had little doubt that he was off to search out his friends who were here. Others who had grown up on the streets with him supported her efforts, more for the good doctor's benefit than hers, she was certain. He seemed to instill loyalty in people. But then that probably wasn't unusual considering his skill at warding off death's advances.

Yet she did often find herself wishing she had met him under different circumstances, that she had met him before she had ever become a wife.

Standing in a darkened corner of the terrace, William Graves sipped the whiskey that he'd pilfered from the library. He preferred the bite of hard liquor to champagne. It was more in line with the darkness that resided inside him.

Dancing with Winifred Buckland, Duchess of Avendale, served as his favorite moments of the year. Even though the activity was pure torment.

Three years ago, he'd done what was necessary to save her, although not everything was exactly legal. Not that he'd ever suffered any guilt over skirting the law. But he wasn't certain she would be as accepting of his wrongdoing. As a matter of fact, he was rather certain she would despise him for his role in her husband's demise, and so he kept his distance when he would prefer to close the gap between them.

Or at least explore the possibility of closing it. He was drawn to her in ways he'd never been drawn to another

woman. She possessed a vulnerability that he suspected hid
a reservoir of strength, and he would dearly love to help her
uncover that secret about herself, but he feared her discovery
of *his* secrets.

His secrets that could very well destroy not only her but
every other soul about whom he cared.

So for two years now, he came to this blasted ball. He
danced once with her. He inhaled her jasmine fragrance,
felt the heat of her skin seeping through her clothes and his
gloves to mingle with the warmth of his hands. He gazed
into her somber brown eyes, and wished to God that he possessed the power to make her laugh. He studied her crooked
nose, which in spite of its origins he found endearing, and
wondered if she were aware how many times she rubbed the
bridge of it, how many times she seemed to try to hide it. He
was familiar with the scar across her eyebrow, the one on her
cheek, and the faint one on the underside of her chin that she
might not even know was there. He found no fault with them,
as they were signs of survival, but he loathed the reasons that
she possessed them.

Still, he often thought of how it would feel to trail his
mouth over them, and wondered if in the process he would
heal the inner hurts with as much success as he'd managed to
heal the outer ones.

He longed to remove the pins from her mahogany hair.
He doubted she was aware that during some of her moments
of delirium he had brushed it to keep it from becoming so
infested with tangles that it would need to be shorn. It fell
to her waist, and was so beautiful. As beautiful as she was.
He could gaze into her brown eyes for hours, but he'd done

all the gazing he allowed himself for the night. One dance. A few moments. He dared not torture himself further by taking more. His ability to resist her was on a weak tether.

He downed the contents of the tumbler before setting it aside on the railing. Time to be off, to find another woman to distract him from his desires. Although unfortunately, since he'd met her, all other women paled in comparison, left him wanting. He often worked himself to exhaustion simply so he wouldn't carry her into dreams, because she never wore a stitch of clothing there, and his frustration with past actions merely increased. But even knowing the price he paid, he would do it again without hesitation. He would do anything at all to protect her.

Turning on his heel, he paused as he saw the duchess descending the steps that led into the garden. He shouldn't follow her. She might have arranged a tryst, but he seemed incapable of stopping his legs from making short work of closing the distance separating them. "Duchess?"

Stopping, she faced him. Within the pale light cast by the gas lamps that lined the path, he saw her slight smile. Gentle, warm, welcoming. She was the kindest person he'd ever known. In his youth he had longed for one kind touch, one sweet caress that would ease all the hurts. He imagined she would be a balm to his harsh soul.

"I do wish you would call me Winnie," she said softly.

"You're a duchess; I'm a commoner."

"A commoner who serves as one of the queen's many physicians. I would say that makes you uncommon, Dr. Graves."

Ignoring her argument—he needed nothing to create a

sense of intimacy between them that might weaken his resolve to remain aloof—he said, "Should you be out here
alone?"

"It's my garden. As a widow, I have no need of a chaper-
one." She looked back over her shoulder. "It's such a crush in
there, which is a great benefit to the cause, but I was beginning to feel as though I were suffocating. I just needed a bit of
fresh air, so I thought to take a quick turn about the garden.
Would you care to join me?"

He knew the correct answer, the safe answer. Instead he
heard himself uttering neither. "I would, very much."

Then he did something equally stupid: he offered her his
arm. She placed her small hand on the crook of his elbow, and
while he wore a shirt and jacket, he could still feel the inden-
tation of each finger through the cloth until he would swear
that she was burning a brand onto his skin. Her head was a
good six inches below his shoulder. She was such a tiny thing,
which made him even angrier when he thought of her brute
of a husband taking his fists to her, before holding her down
and forcing himself on her. He'd gotten what he deserved,
and William had no regrets about it. If it added the weight
of guilt to his own conscience so be it. It wasn't the first time.

A cool breeze wafted through the lovely summer evening, holding the fog at bay. A few other couples were walking about. The whisperings of some who had strayed from
the path mingled with the chirping of insects. The darkness
created an intimacy that made it easy to believe that secrets
could be kept there.

"Why does Victoria require so many physicians?" the
duchess asked.

Because she suffers greatly from hypochondria. Not that he was about to share that information. He did not discuss the ailments of those he attended. "She's the queen and wants to ensure she stays healthy for her subjects. Sometimes it helps to have more than one opinion on a matter. Medicine is not an exact science, and we still have much to learn."

"It must be fascinating, though, to see all that you do."

"Fascinating, heartbreaking. I prefer the days when my patients recover to the days when they don't."

"Strange, but I never consider that you lose patients. I suppose I was so near death when you brought me around that I believe you can accomplish miracles," she said.

"Hardly. I am but a man, not a miracle worker."

They were farther into the garden now, away from the lights, but his eyes had adjusted and he could see clearly where they were going. No other couples seemed to be about. They should turn around. But then he didn't always do the things he should.

"Do you know much about the workings of the brain?" she asked.

"I've managed to remove a tumor or two, quite successfully. Are you experiencing headaches?" He didn't like the notion of her suffering further. She'd experience enough pain at the hands of her husband to last a lifetime, but he was well acquainted with the fact that people didn't always get the carefree existence they deserved.

"No, not at all. It's forgetfulness mostly. It's silly really. I have a sapphire necklace that I'd planned to wear with this gown but when I went to retrieve it from the safe in my bed-chamber, it was gone."

"Stolen, then."

"That's the thing. I don't know. The safe was closed up tight. Who would steal it? The servants have been in my employ for years. Why would they suddenly begin pilfering? Although to be honest, it's more than that single incident. There have been other things happening that have given me cause for concern."

"Such as?"

"It seems that I keep misplacing things. I don't know why I'm so forgetful of late."

He stopped walking, placed his hands on her shoulders, and turned her so she faced him directly. He'd removed his gloves when he'd left the salon in search of stronger drink. It took all his inner strength to not take his palms on a leisurely sojourn over her silken bared skin, not to peel off *her* gloves, not to toy with her hair, not to take advantage of this moment when she was gazing at him with such earnestness. Forcing his errant thoughts back to the matter at hand, he wished he had more light, had his instruments with him so he could examine her eyes more closely. From caring for her before, he was quite familiar with the brown depths, the darker circle around her iris, the small golden flecks that caught the light. "You took quite a blow to the head three years ago. What you're experiencing could be a result of an injury that I failed to properly diagnose."

"But why only now?"

"When did it start?"

She shook her head, and he found himself wishing that her movements would loosen the pins, until her hair escaped its bonds and he could tunnel his fingers through it. Why was it always so hard with her to be the impersonal physician he had been trained to be? He was supposed to look at her as an object to be analyzed, not a woman to be explored.

"Two, three months ago," she said lightly, completely unaware of the turmoil wreaking havoc with him. "Right after I came back to London for the Season. Would damage to my brain take that long to manifest itself?"

He didn't think so, but as he'd told her, the medical community was still learning things about the human condition. "Have you had any other blow to the head recently? Any accident? Have you fallen?"

"No, nothing. And I'm sorry." She laughed lightly, a tinkling of bells that caused his gut to tighten with the memory of the first time he'd heard the sweet sound. She was watching her young son play with Frannie in William's garden, and her delight had given him his first sprig of hope that she would indeed recover, that he had managed to discover every injury that needed tending. But now he had to wonder if he had overlooked something, something vital that might plague her for the remainder of her years. "I didn't mean to cause you undue worry. Tonight is supposed to be for merriment."

But he was concerned. People could appear perfectly fine, but something dark and sinister could be lurking, waiting to snatch away life. In his youth, he'd been far too familiar with dark and sinister, and his fears had led to disaster. No matter how many lives he saved, he could not make amends for the life that had been forfeit because of his weakness. "I want you to come to my office tomorrow for an examination."

"Do you really think that's necessary?"

"I won't know until I have a look. And I'll send word 'round to Inspector Swindler of Scotland Yard. I'm not an expert on safes. They weren't my purview when I lived on the streets, but he should be able to examine yours in order to determine if someone without a key managed to break into it."

"I forgot you were once a thief. I've only heard bits of rumors about your past. Was it horrid?"

"Not all of it." He cradled her face between his hands. A mistake. Her skin was so smooth, like the finest of silk. At her throat, he could feel her pulse thrumming against his fingers. "I want you to promise that you will come see me tomorrow."

"Yes, all right. Is it still the place where you took me all those years ago?"

He couldn't help himself. He skimmed his thumbs over her cheeks. "Yes. I can send a carriage round for you."

"No, I remember where it is. I can find it. What time?"

Tracing the outer line of her lips, he heard her soft intake of breath. "Whatever time works best for you."

She simply nodded, her gaze fastened on him. Considering what he knew of her past, he was surprised that she didn't run screaming back to the residence.

"I don't want you to be afraid, Winnie." He cursed himself for the ease with which her name rolled off his tongue.

"I'm not when I'm with you."

You should be, he thought. God help her, but she should be. Whatever reservoir of control he possessed dissipated.

With a harsh curse echoing between them, he lowered his mouth to hers. Her lips were as plump and soft as he'd always imagined, parting slightly, hesitantly, inviting him to take further liberties. And he was scoundrel enough to accept the invitation.

She moaned as he swept his tongue through her sweet mouth. She tasted of champagne, and he wondered if she were at ease with him because she'd had a few glasses too many. Then his wondering turned to wonder as her tongue explored his mouth with equal fervor. The advantage to being with a widow. She wasn't innocent. God, he knew she was far from that. She clutched the lapels of his jacket. Closing his arms around her, he brought her in closer to him, until her body was pressed against his. He could feel her curves, her dips and swells. He cursed the clothes separating them.

Her nails scraped his scalp just before her fingers trailed along his jaw. Sighing, she wound her arms around his neck, bringing herself in even nearer.

For three years now, he had dreamed of this moment, fantasized about it, envisioned it, but had never dared believe he would ever possess it. He didn't want to give it up, didn't want to stop. He delved deeper, unleashing the hunger he'd held in check—for her, only for her.

She deserved someone far better than he, someone who didn't lie, who didn't hold secrets, who could sit with her before a fire and never fear being honest. But with her, he would always have to watch his words, always take care in what he revealed. She had said she wasn't afraid of him, but he knew that if she understood exactly what he was capable of doing she would be terrified. She wouldn't trust him. He doubted that she would like him; she most certainly would not love him.

Even kissing her had the possibility of leading to disaster— and he wasn't the only one whose life might be ruined. He should pull back now. And he would.

After one more moment.

One more moment of her sighs and moans. One more moment of her lush body writhing against his. One more moment of her arms entwined tightly around him as though she would never let go.

He wanted to undo fastenings. He wanted to lift her into his arms and carry her to her bedchamber. He wanted to do all the things he shouldn't. But indulgences came with a price, and he couldn't in all good conscience ask her to pay it.

With a groan of frustration, he drew back. Releasing quick, short breaths, she stared up at him with expectation. Better to disappoint her now than to risk destroying her. Being too long in his company would not be wise for either of them.

"Goodnight, Duchess." Pivoting abruptly on his heel, he strode toward the back gate that would lead him into the mews. For a few moments, he had experienced heaven, and he knew without doubt that he would spend the remaining hours of his night languishing in the depths of hell.

CHAPTER TWO

As Winnie strolled back into the ballroom, she wondered if anyone would notice that her eyes were just a tad brighter, her lips a bit swollen, her skin slightly flushed. Without looking in a mirror, she knew all that was true because she felt as though she had changed in the space of a few moments, had morphed into someone with a spring in her step, a lightness in her soul that she had never experienced before.

Avendale had kissed her, but without tenderness or gentleness. Even as passion had begun to take hold and William had deepened the kiss, it wasn't about possession or control, but rather giving, sharing, enjoying—completely and absolutely. While she had initially been taken aback by his hunger, had experienced a few seconds of panic, his tenacity, his honest desire had enticed her to react in kind, to know that he meant her no harm. He caused her heart to accelerate, her skin to warm, her nerves to tingle, her toes to curl. In a few breathless moments he had shown her that it could be pleasant to have a man's attentions.

He had kissed her tonight and she would see him on the

morrow. She could scarcely wait. It didn't matter that he had left abruptly or that he had not used an endearment as they parted ways. What mattered was that she knew he desired her. What mattered was that he didn't frighten her.

"Winnie?"

She came to a quick stop as her dearest friend in all the world, the Countess of Claybourne, approached her. "Hello, Catherine."

Catherine had given her a quick hug and a kiss on the cheek when she and the Earl of Claybourne had arrived earlier. Now she simply studied Winnie as though seeing her for the first time. "You appear happy."

"Yes." She dearly wanted to tell her why, but it was still so fresh, so wonderful that she decided to hold it to herself for a while longer, to simply embrace the amazement and glow of it. "I have every reason to be. The ball is quite the success."

"Do you remember how hard I had to work to convince you that you could throw a smashing party?"

Winnie nodded, with the reminder of how she had fretted over the balls she'd given while Avendale was alive. "But I no longer have a fear of disappointing anyone. William Graves is most appreciative. He and I are going to meet later in the week to discuss the plans for the hospital." She saw no reason to mention that she would also see him on the morrow. She had no desire to worry her friend, and in all likelihood nothing was wrong. Perhaps it was little more than being distracted arranging this affair. Yes, that was it, she was certain. She began planning it as soon as she arrived in London. She wanted everything to be perfect. She was devoted to it, and so her mind had been unable to focus on anything else.

"That's wonderful," Catherine said now about the hospital. "I'm so glad you have this project to occupy your time."

"I rather enjoy it, meeting with the architects and builders. William Graves has given me leave to design it however I'd like. I've gone through tours of other hospitals, spoken with staff so I have a better understanding of all that is needed. I believe Dr. Graves will be pleased with my efforts."

"I'm certain he will be. I'm quite impressed." Reaching out, touching the petal of a lily sitting in a large blue vase, Catherine said, "Speaking of Graves, I saw you waltzing with him earlier."

"You look as though something is afoot when you know he always dances with me. One dance. One dance only. I suppose it's his way of thanking me."

"You like him."

"He's very kind as you're well aware."

Catherine gave her a concerned smile. "Just take care, sweetling. His work comes first and always will. He's dedicated to his patients."

An hour ago, half an hour ago, Winnie would have simply nodded in agreement—but William Graves had kissed her. "I'm not expecting anything of him." Well, perhaps she was just a little.

At that moment, the Earl of Claybourne appeared to claim his wife for a dance. Winnie had never expected Catherine to marry the Devil Earl, but she couldn't deny that her friend was incredibly happy, and that the man obviously adored her.

The remainder of the evening, she visited with one person after another, ensured that food and champagne were readily available, thanked people for supporting her event, for ensuring that a first-rate hospital would be built. By the time midnight rolled around and everyone had left, she was exhausted from serving as hostess. She had to fairly drag herself up the stairs. But she couldn't go to bed just yet.

Walking past her bedchamber, she carried on to one three doors down. Inside, she found her seven-year-old son sprawled over his bed, snoring lightly. The door to his governess's apartments was closed as he was getting old enough not to be watched every moment. A lamp burned low on the table beside his bed. He'd never liked sleeping in the dark.

She approached as quietly as possible, then softly brushed his brown hair back from his brow. With his father's death, he became the Duke of Avendale but she couldn't quite bring herself to call him by his rightful title, perhaps because it still reminded her too much of her husband. To her, her son was Whit, the name that had become his while he held the courtesy title of the Earl of Whitson. She also believed *Whit* seemed more appropriate for a child. She suspected it wouldn't be too long before he would begin wanting to be called by the name that had belonged to his father. But until then, she would have things her way.

She could only be grateful that his father had never taken a hand to him, that Whit had been too young to understand all that was happening within this household. And while she was certain that she would go to hell, she wouldn't feel guilty about being glad that her husband had died. She knew it made her an awful person, but not nearly as dreadful as Avendale had been.

Leaning down, she pressed a light kiss to Whit's forehead. "Sweet dreams, my love."

She stilled as a fragrance assailed her. Caraway. It was a scent she associated with her husband, with pain, with humiliation. Her heart pounding, she spun around and searched the shadows. She saw nothing but the veiled darkness.

She was being ridiculous. Avendale was dead, but of late, the smell of him had begun seeping out of corners, out of little pockets, catching her unawares from time to time. She forbade the servants from having caraway seeds in the residence, from indulging in eating them. Someone must be disobeying the edict. She would have to take the matter up with the butler on the morrow.

She wanted no reminders of her husband, nothing that dredged up memories of her miserable existence while she had lived under his thumb.

With one last look at Whit, she silently left the room, closing the door quietly behind her. Her heart was finally returning to its normal rhythm. Perhaps it was time to find another residence in London. This one contained far too many memories. Wherever she looked, she saw reminders of Avendale. It made little sense that she would begin to smell him, as it had been three years since his passing, but his habit of constantly chewing on caraway seeds had caused the fragrance to permeate everything. When the house was closed up for winter, perhaps the scent had been trapped in little pockets of air and was released as the house was opened back up. But why had she not noticed it here sooner? She couldn't explain it, didn't want to think about it anymore.

After arriving in her bedchamber, she rung for her lady's maid. It seemed to take no time at all for Sarah to prepare her for bed. After the servant left, Winnie studied her reflection in the mirror at the dressing table. From a certain angle, it was almost impossible to tell that her nose had been broken. She flinched at the memory of the pain, the blood, the crack of cartilage giving way beneath the meaty fist. Her offense had been allowing the Devil Earl to attend their ball. Her husband had been furious.

She hadn't run images of that horrid night through her mind in a good long while. She did hope she wouldn't awaken in a cold sweat with her screams echoing through the room. Thoughts of that night so often brought on nightmares, even though years had passed. It was as though they were woven into the fabric of her soul.

Rising from the chair, she gave her reflection one last look before wandering over to the bed. As she crawled between the sheets, she had a momentary vision of William Graves waiting for her there, of his taking her into his arms, and kissing her with the same passion that he had in the garden. While she had every reason to dread the intimacy that would follow, she found herself anticipating it. She fully understood that not all men were as brutish as Avendale. She longed to glow with the happiness that Catherine did.

She didn't bother to reach for the lamp, to extinguish the flame. Her son wasn't the only one who didn't want to sleep in the dark.

Rolling onto her side, she slipped a hand beneath the pillow—

Froze as her fingers touched something hard and cold.

No, it couldn't be. It wasn't possible.

Straightening, she flung the pillow aside and gasped at the sight of the sapphire necklace winking up at her.

Sitting in a chair in front of the fireplace in his small private parlor, William Graves slowly sipped his whiskey. He'd known sleep wouldn't come easily tonight, not after indulging himself. He could still taste Winnie on his tongue, could still feel the impression of her body pressed against his. Devil take him, but he was a fool to yearn for something he could never possess.

He generally called on his patients, except for those he saw in hospital. Winifred Buckland had been the first he'd nurtured back to health in his residence. It had been a strange thing, having her in his home. It had seemed not quite so empty, so lonely.

While she had been here, after caring for a patient, he anticipated returning to his residence. His first order of business was to look in on her—regardless of the hour. Sometimes he would watch as she endured a restless sleep that even laudanum couldn't tame. He would hold her hand, one that was neither rough nor callused, and urge her to fight. When she had begun to recover, he had spent hours talking with her. Day by day, he observed as she grew stronger not only in body, but in spirit. He caught glimpses of the lady she might have been before her marriage, and he was intrigued by the certainty of her demeanor that began to rise to the fore. It was then that she started discussing her plans to build a hospital as a way to repay him for his kindness. He loved the way her eyes sparkled when she spoke of different aspects she planned to include. Her excitement was contagious, and for the first time in his life, he'd wondered if he had punished himself enough, if he were finally deserving of love.

His musings were interrupted by a knock at his door. He thought nothing of it as he was accustomed to visitors at all hours of the night. The arrival of illness and injuries were not dictated by the ticking of a clock. With haste, he set aside his tumbler, got up, and marched to the door. Opening it, he stared at his visitor. "Winnie?"

"I need to talk to you straightaway."

A pelisse was draped over her shoulders. Her hair was braided. If not for the trepidation in her features, he might have been distracted by thoughts of unraveling the strands. "Yes, of course, come in."

As she stepped through the portal, he caught a glimpse of her carriage in the street. The fog was beginning to roll in. All seemed quiet, but then considering the hour he hadn't expected anything else. Closing the door, he led her into the parlor. "Please sit down."

She took a chair near the fire. Kneeling in front of her, he took her hands. He could feel the tiny tremors cascading through her. "My God, you're like ice."

"I didn't know where else to come." She lifted tear filled eyes to him. "I believe I'm going mad."

"Why ever would you think that?"

Pulling her hands free of his, she reached into her reticule, removed something, then slowly unfurled her fingers to reveal a necklace of sapphires. "I found it beneath my pillow."

"You're going to tell me everything, but first we have to stop your trembling."

Straightening, he went to a table set against a wall and poured whiskey into a glass. He wished he had something a bit more elegant for her, but as he rarely had visitors other than those seeking he come with them posthaste, he didn't bother with having an assortment of liquor on hand. Whiskey served his needs and when people were upset and in want of something more than his words, it usually served theirs.

He had invited her to come here for an examination because he had an examination room here, and he'd thought she'd be more comfortable talking candidly away from her residence. It harbored far too many bad memories.

He crossed back over and handed her the glass. With a grateful nod, she took his offering and sipped. He suspected she was too upset to fully take notice of the fire going down, but hopefully it would serve to warm her.

Taking the chair opposite hers, he studied her for a moment. She was pale, far too pale, although he could see a hint of color returning to her cheeks. He understood now why her hair was braided. Having found the item beneath her pillow, she had no doubt retired for the night. He fought not to distract himself with images of her in the bed.

"Now tell me about the necklace," he urged quietly.

"I told you about it in the garden, how it wasn't in the safe. As I was settling into bed, I slipped my hand beneath the pillow. I discovered it there. Why would anyone put it there?"

Leaning forward, elbows on thighs, he worked to think things through. He wasn't nearly as good with this deciphering motives business as Swindler. He was better at determining the cause of fevers, illnesses, and injuries. "Perhaps someone had taken it from the safe, heard you coming, and slipped it under the pillow to retrieve later."

"A servant? Why would they begin stealing from me now?"

"Gambling debts, perhaps. Maybe they fell in with a rough lot on their day off."

"I'm afraid I did it." She rubbed her brow. "As I mentioned in the garden, I've experienced some bouts of forgetfulness. I've been misplacing a lot of things lately. A book on the table beside my bed. I use a ribbon to mark my place. Sometimes when I open the book to the ribbon, it's either at a place I've read before or a place pages away from where I finished. My perfume atomizer. I keep it on my dressing table. But once I found it on the windowsill."

"Easily explained. A servant not taking care as she's cleaning."

She shook her head vigorously. "Sometimes when I wake up at night, I smell my husband. He had a penchant for eating caraway seeds incessantly. He always smelled of them. I've forbidden the servants from having them in the residence. But the odor is sometimes there in different places. I also sleep with a lamp burning, but sometimes I will awaken to absolute darkness, the flame extinguished, the caraway scent more vivid as though I've had a visitor."

She folded her hands so tightly around the glass he could see the whites of her knuckles. It was not to be tolerated. He shot out of the chair, knelt before her, took the glass, and once again wrapped his hands around hers. "Fragrances linger, particularly in cloth. I have a handkerchief that belonged to my father. I can still smell him in it."

"I considered that, but Dr. Graves—"

"Please call me Bill."

"It's too harsh. I prefer William."

"William it is." He preferred it as well, but his friends

had always called him Bill and on the streets it was a stronger name, one that bespoke confidence. He skimmed his thumbs over her knuckles. "I'm sure there is a simple explanation for everything."

"Yes, quite. As I said I'm going mad."

"I seriously doubt that."

"Then perhaps his ghost is haunting me, because I could swear that I have seen him."

Every muscle and fiber of his being stood at attention. "Where?"

"Once at the far end of the garden. At twilight. It was difficult to see very clearly, because the shadows were moving in. He was there and then he wasn't. Another time in the park. Although I can't be absolutely sure as he was so far away, but the resemblance at a distance was uncanny. In truth, though, it wasn't so much the sight of him as it was the sense of him watching me. I could always feel when Avendale watched me, because he did it with such intensity as though he expected me to make a mistake or behave badly, and he wanted to be able to pounce immediately in order to correct me."

He lifted his hand to her cheek and slowly stroked the soft skin. "My mother was an unkind woman who beat me religiously. When she passed, for years, I thought I saw her in the streets. I still think I see her from time to time—especially those nights when I'm exhausted and my guard is down. When we are traumatized by those whom we love, it's often difficult to believe they are actually gone. But your husband is gone. He can't hurt you, Winnie."

She nodded. "I know, and you could not have spoken truer words. It is frightfully difficult to believe sometimes that he is truly gone—which brings me back to the possibility that perhaps I am going mad. Because I sense his presence when I know I shouldn't."

"Winnie, you need to dispense with this notion that you're going mad. You survived a horrendous ordeal that most would find difficult if not impossible to overcome. The remnants of it, not the ghost of your husband, are haunting you. But you will survive this. You need to ensure you get plenty of rest and that you have things to occupy your time and your mind so you aren't becoming lost in the past."

As she smiled, the guilt ricocheted through him. "Like the hospital," she said.

"Yes. We'll get together to discuss it in a couple of days. But now it's late and you should get some much-needed rest."

She laid her hand against his cheek. "Thank you so much. You always make me feel better."

Holding her hand in place, he turned his head slightly and pressed a kiss to her palm. "It's my pleasure. I'll see you home."

"It's not necessary. I've already disturbed you enough."

"You never disturb me."

He banked the fire and grabbed his jacket before escorting her out to the waiting carriage. After assisting her inside, he sat beside her, placed his arm around her shoulders, and drew her in against his side. Everything within him screamed that it wasn't appropriate. But then it was the time of night for inappropriate things. He placed his lips on the top of her head, took what joy he could from her nearness.

"I feel like such a ninny," she said after a while. "I don't know how I reacted as I did. I'm sure there is a logical explanation for everything."

"You're not a ninny. Sometimes we just need to talk with someone about the things bothering us. We can blow them out of proportion if we are our only counsel."

"You're always so kind."

No, not always. He suspected her husband would describe him as the devil.

The carriage came to a halt. He alighted then handed her down. "I would like to take a stroll through your residence just to assure you that there are no monsters lurking in the corners."

"I feel like a child."

"You're not. Oftentimes, we need assurances."

She gave him a sweet smile. "All right then."

She unlocked the door. As they went in, he found some relief in the fact that she had locked the door before she left. But it might be worth it to have the locks changed. He'd mention it later. He didn't want to alarm her any more than she was already alarmed.

Leaving her in the foyer, he walked briskly through rooms that in no way reminded him of her. While no longer here, her husband's presence was overbearing in dark, sturdy furniture, dark walls, thick draperies. He took an extra moment in a small room that he had no doubt served not only as her sitting room, but her sanctuary. A delicate secretary stood against a wall, fragile animal figurines adorned small tables. The fabric covering the chairs and sofa were pale yellow and green, as though she'd been striving to bring sunshine into her life. Above the fireplace was a painting of a young girl with a basket of flowers. The eyes were innocent, but he would have recognized them anywhere. They belonged to Winnie.

But he found nothing suspicious among the shadows in any of the rooms.

He gave her a reassuring nod when he met back up with her in the foyer. "All seems to be in order down here," he assured her.

He escorted her up the stairs. While she waited outside her bedchamber door, he examined her room, making note of the tiniest of details: the blue flowers on the wall paper, the rumpled bed linens, the copy of *Oliver Twist* on the bedside table. Her exotic jasmine fragrance permeating the room. A gilded-framed painting of a small boy plucking flowers. Behind it, he was certain he would find her safe where she thought her most precious jewels would be secure.

He stepped back into the hallway. "All seems to be in order. I'm just going to dash through the other rooms."

He made short work of the task, taking care not to awaken her son. As a boy, working for Feagan, he had learned how to break into homes and assess the inside quickly to find the treasurers. Some skills one never forgot.

As he returned to her side, she blushed. "No ghosts?" she asked.

"None that I could detect."

"Truth be told, I didn't truly expect you to find anything. It's all so odd, isn't it?"

"I'm sure there's an explanation. We'll figure it out easily enough. Meanwhile, try to get some sleep and send word if you need me—for anything."

"I truly appreciate your kindness and assistance. I've instructed my driver to return you to your residence."

"Thank you." Cradling her face with one hand, he leaned

in and kissed her, just a brief taste to sustain him for what he had to do next. "Sweet dreams, Winnie."

Leaving her there, he hurried down the stairs before bad judgment overtook him and he found himself putting her to bed—and ensuring he joined her there to rumple those bed linens a bit more. He was loath to leave her, but he knew no good would come of his staying.

Once outside, he called up to the driver, "Carry on. I'll be walking."

He waited until the carriage disappeared up the drive on its way to the carriage house. Then he took a quick turn about the gardens. Nothing amiss. No one hiding in the shadows. He tried to take some comfort from that.

But he found there was none to be had.

An hour later he was standing by the fireplace within the Earl of Claybourne's library. Claybourne and his wife were nestled on a couch together. Frannie Mabry, the Duchess of Greystone, sat in a wingback chair near the one in which Jack Dodger lounged. James Swindler had taken a seat at the outer edge of the circle.

"It's half past three in the morning. What the devil is going on?" Claybourne asked.

"We may have a problem," Graves told him.

"What the deuce would that be?"

"The Duke of Avendale. I fear he may have risen from the dead."

CHAPTER THREE

Silence greeted his pronouncement, which didn't surprise him in the least. They'd all played a role in Avendale's "death." Graves had provided the charred remains of a corpse, identified as the duke only because it wore the duke's rings.

"Are you quite certain that he was sent to the penal colony in New Zealand?" Graves asked.

"I saw him dragged onto the prison hulk myself," Claybourne said. He was the one who had captured Avendale, broken his jaw so he couldn't speak, and delivered him into Swindler's keeping. "Catherine was with me. She can attest to it."

Beside him, his wife looked as though she might be ill. She had conveyed the news to her dear friend that her husband had perished in a fire at Heatherwood. "We stayed until the ship left port."

"Is it possible that he found a way to escape and return here?" Graves asked.

"Anything's possible," Swindler said. Working for Scotland Yard, he had access to the gaols and prisons. He had found a fourteen-year-old lad sentenced to transportation to a prison colony. He substituted Avendale for the boy.

"His sentence was for life, on the far side of the world," Frannie pointed out. As a child, she'd been fascinated with letters and numbers, endlessly copying them until she could create any style, which made her an excellent forger. She had altered the documents so the description of the person sentenced more closely resembled Avendale. "How would he have managed to find his way back here?"

"He's a bloody duke," Jack reminded them. He had provided employment and a safe haven for the boy they had liberated when they tossed Avendale into the gaol as his replacement. "Once he healed enough to speak coherently, he could offer a fortune to someone willing to help him. As I was not here when you all made the decision to go forward with this swindle, I can't attest to how well thought out it might have been."

"It was very well thought out," Claybourne said. He turned his attention to William. "All this conjecture seems rather pointless. Why do you think he's returned?"

"Because Winnie—" He stopped, cleared his throat. "The Duchess of Avendale believes she's seen him."

Catherine gasped, placing her hand over her mouth. "No, it can't be. He'll kill her this time."

Suddenly Graves was concerned he was raising the alarm a bit prematurely. It did seem unlikely that the man could escape and make his way back here. "She can't be sure. She saw him at a distance, thought it was a ghost. But there are other things. Items being moved around. His scent wafting through the house. Things she can't explain."

"She's told me none of this."

"She feared she was going mad."

"Perhaps she is," Jack said. "If he did manage to return, I think he would march into his residence and announce that he had bloody well returned."

"No," Catherine said quietly. "I think he would strive to take his revenge by driving her mad. At least for a time. He's had three years to ponder retribution. He's the sort who enjoys pulling wings off flies rather than smashing them."

Claybourne placed his hand over hers. "Do you want to tell the duchess what we did?"

Slowly, Catherine shook her head. "She would never forgive me. As horrible as he was, she wept when I told her that he died. As for the rest of you, if she told anyone of any consequence, you would all be ruined, possibly imprisoned. No, we swore three years ago that we would bear the burden of it and it would remain our secret. We must keep to that vow. But how do we protect her if we don't tell her that she's in need of protection?"

"We could be getting ahead of ourselves here," Swindler said. "First, we need to discover if he is in fact here. I would like to have a look through her house."

"I've actually put something into play," Graves said. He explained about the sapphires and the safe. "She won't be surprised when I bring you 'round to examine the safe."

"We'll need more than that," Claybourne said. "We'll need you to spend more time with her."

"Jack has brutes he can send over to keep watch on the residence," Graves said.

"The outside of it, yes. But as it appears Avendale may be

lurking about inside, we need someone inside to watch and, if needed, to protect her. As the rest of us gents are married, I'm afraid it falls to you."

Not precisely what Graves wanted to hear. As their earlier walk in the garden had proven, his desire for her was on a weak tether. Her husband had taken atrocious advantage of her. Graves had no wish to put himself in the same league, but everything he'd worked so hard to attain was at risk.

"Do we need to be concerned that he'll hurt the boy?" Frannie asked.

"His heir?" Catherine questioned. "Not likely. He had two other wives before Winnie and neither produced a child, so I suspect he won't risk Whit. He never hurt him before. His preferred target seems to be women."

"What happened to his other wives?" Swindler asked. Graves wasn't surprised that he had homed in on that particular aspect of Catherine's words. The man was a demon for justice.

"They died," Catherine said. "One took a tumble down the stairs, the other a fatal blow to the head when she fell from her bed."

"Where was the bed?" Swindler asked. "On the roof?"

Catherine gave a hint of smile. "You understand now the depth of our concerns. If he is here, he will try to destroy us in his own manner—no matter how long it takes or what is required."

While Graves was a man dedicated to saving lives, he could not help but believe that they would all have been better served if Claybourne had simply killed Avendale when presented with the opportunity. Now far too many people could be made to suffer.

Winnie most of all.

Winnie thought she should be terrified of the huge hulk of a man who stood in her entryway, but there was a gentleness in his smile that was reassuring. It also helped that William stood beside him. She was familiar with Inspector James Swindler. He had quite the reputation for solving crimes, but they had never been formally introduced as they were now.

"Bill says you've had a bit of a problem with items disappearing from your safe. I'd like to examine it."

"Yes, of course. It's in my bedchamber."

He held up a finger. "When we get there, don't tell me where it is. Allow me the fun of ferreting it out for myself."

As she climbed the stairs, Swindler followed behind while William walked beside her.

"He's very good at what he does," William said.

"So I've heard, although I do find his notion of what constitutes fun a bit odd."

William chuckled low. "He loves solving a good mystery, even if it's little more than searching for a safe."

"Well, I do hope he solves our mystery quite quickly. I couldn't relax enough to go to sleep after I returned here last night."

She led them into her bedchamber. William stood beside her while Swindler stepped into the room, gave a quick glance around, and walked straight over to a painting, lifted the frame off the nail, and revealed the safe.

"How did you know?" she asked, as he leaned the painting against the wall. "There are other pictures about."

"Yes, but they were placed with the intent of complementing the décor of the room. This one was placed to hide something, so it looks slightly out of place. Who all has a key?" he asked as he reached into his coat pocket and withdrew a small pouch. Opening it, he removed a couple of long, slender instruments.

"Only I do."

"None of the servants? No one else?"

"No."

"Has anyone else ever possessed the key?"

"Only my husband."

He and William exchanged a glance.

"But he's dead," she felt compelled to add.

"Do you know where his key is?"

She rubbed her forehead, where an ache was beginning to take hold. "No, I don't. I went through his belongings, but I don't recall seeing it."

"So someone might have taken it," he answered distractedly as he worked the instruments into the keyhole. She heard a snap and the door opened a crack. He opened it further. "A rather simple lock system. Anyone could have broken into it."

"And relocked it?" William asked.

"That might have proven tricky. We'll see about replacing this with something that will guard your valuables better."

"I suppose there is some comfort in knowing anyone could have run off with it," she said. "But why didn't they?"

Swindler shrugged. "That I can't answer, Your Grace. Bill says you don't suspect your servants, so it's quite possible someone managed to get inside without anyone seeing. We'll want to change the locks on all the doors as well."

"Yes, all right. Have you had other reports of incidents such as this?"

"Something similar, yes. But not to worry, Scotland Yard is on it."

Swindler left, but William stayed, suggesting that Winnie show him the plans for the hospital she'd mentioned the night before. She took him to her study. It was much smaller than Avendale's, the furniture more dainty. It looked out on the gardens. With the draperies pulled back, sunlight poured in. She'd never felt comfortable in Avendale's library. Everything was so dark, the furniture bold and intimidating.

"After the success of last year's ball, I took the liberty of hiring an architect." She went behind the desk, picked up a scroll, and began rolling it across the top of her desk. "I know I might have been a bit premature—"

"It's fine, Duchess. You're providing the funds. You can handle the building of the hospital however you wish."

He came to stand behind her, looking over her shoulder. Good God, he was so wonderfully tall that he was probably peering over the top of her head. She arranged a marble paperweight on one corner of the parchment. Leaning over, he reached toward an inkwell. She was acutely aware of the press of his chest to her back, the curve of his body around hers. Very slowly, as though they had the remainder of their lives, he set the glass container on the opposite corner of the scroll.

Then placed his hand on the other corner to stop it from curling up.

"That should be all we need," he said quietly, and she felt the brush of his warm breath across her temple.

She could think of a good deal more that she needed: a touch, a kiss, a caress. Rubbing the bridge of her nose, she fought to concentrate on the lines spread out before her. "I'm not sure of all the details, but it has surgical rooms and a separate area for isolating those who are contagious."

"I like that idea. What do you think of having a separate wing for children? It seems as though they should have their own area."

She felt a tiny bubble of joy burst within her chest. Avendale had never asked her opinion on anything. He'd always told her how things were to be. She especially liked that William was thinking of the little ones. "It's a splendid notion. I think it should be right here." She placed her finger on the far end of the building. He wrapped his hand around it.

"I can think of no place better."

Her voice tried to lodge in her throat but she wouldn't have it. She wanted to speak to him, she wanted to tell him everything. "And gardens. Lovely gardens where people can walk as they're recovering. I remember the walks you would take me on, insisting I needed them to regain my strength." Hesitating to say the next words, she swallowed hard. Avendale would have laughed at such silliness, but William wasn't Avendale. Still, if he laughed, she would be incredibly hurt. But she had to risk it. She had tried to shape herself into what Avendale wanted and failed miserably. She needed someone who accepted her as she was. "They became my favorite part of the day."

Tenderly, he curled his hand below her chin and turned her face toward him until he was able to capture her gaze. "They were my favorite part of the day as well."

She didn't know quite what to say to that admission. After last night, she'd dared to hope that she meant something special to him, but they were so very different in rank and purpose. She considered suggesting that they go for a walk now, but she didn't want to move away from where she was. So near to him. He smelled of sandalwood. His jaw and cheeks were smooth. He'd shaved before he came to see her. His hair curled wildly about his head, and she wondered if he ever tried to tame it, then decided he wouldn't look like himself without the wildness.

With his thumb, he stroked her lower lip. His blue eyes darkened. She watched the muscles of his throat work as he swallowed. Leaning in, he lowered his mouth to hers. She rose up on her toes to meet him, inviting him to possess, plunder, have his way. She became lost in the sensations of his mouth playing over hers, vaguely aware of his twisting her around so they were facing each other. As she skimmed her hands up over his shoulders, his arms came around her, drawing her nearer. He was a man of nimble fingers, skilled hands that eased hurts and injuries and warded off death. He had mended her with those hands, and now with his lips he was mending her further.

Suddenly changing the angle of his mouth, he deepened the kiss, his tongue hungrily exploring, enticing her to take her own journey of discovery. He tasted of peppermint. She could well imagine him keeping the hard candies in his pocket to hand to children in order to ease their fears. Snitching one for himself every now and then.

He folded his hands around the sides of her waist and, without breaking his mouth from hers, lifted her onto the desk. Parchment crackled beneath her. She knew she should be worried that they were ruining the plans for the hospital, but she seemed unable to care about anything beyond the wondrous sensations that he was bringing to life.

Avendale had never kissed her with such enthusiasm, such resolve. She felt as though William were determined to devour her, and that it would be one of the most wondrous experiences of her life.

Hiking her skirts up over her knees, he wedged himself between her thighs. Very slowly, he lowered her back to the desk until she was sprawled over it like some wanton. On the desk! She had never known this sort of activity could occur anywhere other than the bed. It was wicked, exciting, intriguing. Surely he didn't mean to do more than kiss her, not that she was opposed to him going further.

She'd gone so long without a caress, without being desired, without having passions stirred. She felt at once terrified and joyful while pleasure curled through her.

As he dragged his mouth along her throat, he began undoing buttons, giving himself access to more skin. He nipped at her collarbone, circled his tongue in the hollow at her throat. She plowed her fingers through his golden locks, relishing the soft curls as they wound around her fingers.

More buttons were unfastened. She sighed as he trailed

his mouth and tongue along the upper swells of her breasts. Heat pooled deep within her. She wrapped her legs around his hips, taking surcease from the pressure of him against her. He moaned low, more a growl than anything as he pressed a kiss in the dip between her breasts.

God help her, but she wanted to feel his touch over all of her.

Peeling back her bodice, he began loosening the ribbons on her chemise. In the distance, someplace far far away, she thought she heard a door open.

"The count—" Her butler began and stopped.

"Winnie?" Catherine's voice brought her crashing back to reality.

Mortified, Winnie knew the heat scorching her now had nothing to do with passion.

William calmly lifted his head. "Excuse us, but she'll need a moment."

A moment? Dear God, she'd need the remainder of her life to get past the humiliation of being caught sprawled over her desk with a man who was not her husband licking at her flesh. She was vaguely aware of the snick of the door closing.

Very slowly, very carefully, as though she were delicate crystal that could easily shatter, William placed his hands beneath her back and helped her sit up. Then closing his arms around her, he held her near, and she buried her face against his chest.

How could his heart beat so methodically when hers was jumping all around, bouncing off her ribs?

"You've done nothing wrong," William said quietly. "Although you might instruct your butler that he needs to knock before entering."

She nodded jerkily. "I want to die."

"Winnie, you are not at fault here. The fault is mine for being unable to resist your charms." He tucked his finger beneath her chin and titled her head back until he was gazing into her eyes. "Invite me to dinner."

"Dinner?"

"Yes, you know. That meal that takes place in the evening, a few hours before bedtime."

"Are you not at all embarrassed by being caught?"

"I've been caught for worst offenses, and there's no punishment to be had here except for the abrupt ending to something that I was enjoying immensely." He gave her a wicked smile. "I'll promise to behave this evening if it'll put you at ease."

As wrong as it was, she wasn't certain she wanted him to behave. Still, she nodded. "Yes, please join me for dinner."

"I'll be here at half past seven." Leaning in, he took her mouth hotly, but swiftly, before giving her a seductive wink and grin. "Now button up."

As he began striding from the room, she slid off the desk and began to do as he suggested.

Catherine Langdon, Countess of Claybourne, paced the hallway just outside the door to Winnie's study. The butler's announcement of her arrival was only a formality that he insisted upon. She knew the duchess would always be at home to her, as did the butler, so she had merely followed him into the study. She should not have been surprised by what greeted her. William Graves might have been a respected physician, but he was also a man, a man whose friendship with her husband had been forged during their youth. She knew the upbringing they'd had and their dislike of convention. But Winnie had always been so terribly proper.

But then so had Catherine upon a time. Scoundrels tended to have their way.

The door to the study opened. Graves closed it behind him and acknowledged her. "Countess." Then, with long strides, he carried on down the hallway as though that were sufficient.

She hurried after him. "What the devil were you doing in there?" Catherine demanded.

He spun around, and she was taken aback by the anger burning in his blue eyes. "If you have to ask then Claybourne is not the man I thought he was."

Obviously he'd not appreciated being interrupted, but the truth of it was that there should have been nothing going on to interrupt. "I know very well *what* you were doing. I was asking why you were doing it."

"I was doing as ordered, ensuring that the lady would want to keep me close."

She took a step forward. "You cannot toy with her affections."

"You can't have it both ways, Countess. Either you tell her why she needs to have someone watching over her or I provide her with a reason to want to keep me near."

"And when the reason no longer exists?"

"We'll deal with the aftermath. I promise it won't be worse than a hangman's noose."

Spinning on his heel, he strode toward the door. She wanted to call after him, wanted to demand more of him, that he not hurt Winnie. But the only way to ensure that would be to do as he suggested: tell Winnie the truth.

Her friend would despise her. She might even decide that Avendale should be welcomed home. Then all would be for naught. She would again be at the mercy of a brute. And those who had been involved in his false demise could very well be introduced to prison or, as Graves had implied, the hangman's noose.

Catherine had worked too hard to protect Winnie from Avendale to see it all undone now. All she could do was hope that they were mistaken about the man being about.

Sitting at a small table on the terrace with Catherine, Winnie ordered the butler to have tea and biscuits brought out. She had retied every ribbon, secured every button, and yet she still felt slightly askew. Every now and then a few strands of her hair would blow across her face with the gentle breeze. No matter how many times she tucked them back into her bun, they came free, reminding her of the madness that had consumed her within her tiny study.

She could taste peppermint on her lips, smell sandalwood on her skin. Her tea sat untouched and cooling because she didn't want to lose the taste of William.

She could only be grateful that it hadn't been Whit who had walked in on them, but she'd had the foresight to send him on an outing to the zoological gardens with his governess that morning. She hadn't wanted him to be about when the inspector arrived. The last thing she desired was for her son to become frightened or to have any doubt regarding his mother's sanity.

"Win, I know it's none of my business—"

"If you're about to comment on what you walked in on, then I quite agree that it is not your business."

Winnie wasn't certain she'd ever seen Catherine's eyes so large with surprise, but then she'd never been one to stand up for herself. However, those days of cowering were behind her. She had nothing to fear any longer. Except for a possible thief or a bout of forgetfulness.

"He's a commoner," Catherine said.

"I've had an aristocrat, thank you very much. And that wasn't so jolly."

"I just don't want you to get hurt," Catherine said.

Reaching out, Winnie squeezed her friend's hand. "I know you mean well. But he's always been kind to me."

"Just don't misinterpret his kindness. Because of your past you're vulnerable."

Shaking her head, she looked out over the gardens. "I used to fear everything. I believed my opinion didn't matter. I thought I was unworthy. I dreaded hosting balls or dinner parties, because I always disappointed Avendale. Now I can do so much more because I've no one to disappoint. William enjoyed the ball. He likes my plans for the hospital. He doesn't judge me, Catherine. He accepts me as I am."

"I didn't realize you knew each other so well."

She gave a secretive smile. "While I was healing he always there. He brushed my hair once. I was fevered and I think he thought I was unaware of my surroundings, but I was afraid if

I let him know that he would stop. A man brushing my hair. I may have begun to fall in love with him then."

"Just take care, sweetling. Like Claybourne, Jack, and Jim, he is a scoundrel at heart."

"And I've yet to hear any of their wives complain."

Chapter Four

Arriving a little before half past seven, Graves circled the grounds to ensure that no one was lurking about. The threat of rain was in the air. He suspected it would arrive before they finished dinner.

After a footman opened the door for him, he waited in the foyer while the butler informed Her Grace of his presence. When he saw Winnie descending the stairs in a lilac gown that revealed bared shoulders, he knew coming this evening was mistake. He should have simply sat on the steps and kept an eye out, because all he wanted now was to carry her back up the stairs to her bedchamber.

Knowing the truth of her situation, he couldn't in all good conscience offer her marriage, knowing it would make her a bigamist. But it didn't stop him from wanting her. Her hair was plaited and twisted in some elaborate design, but his fingers were nimble enough that he could have the pins scattered on the floor and her hair tumbling around her in two seconds. The fastenings on the back of her gown might take four, her corset six. He forced such tempting calculations from his mind as they served no purpose other than to add to his frustration.

She was under his care, and he had a strict moral code when it came to his professional pursuits, but his desire saw the ruse for what it was and refused to cooperate. She wasn't a patient, she wasn't ill. She was someone who intrigued him.

As she neared, her jasmine scent filled his nostrils and he wanted to seek out all the little spots where she applied the fragrance.

"Would you care for a bit of brandy before dinner?" she asked.

What he wanted was an entire bottle of whiskey, or perhaps a dose of laudanum, to drown out his errant thoughts. With a practiced smile that he knew appeared harmless, he shook his head. "You're intoxicating enough."

She laughed joyfully and sweetly. "Rubbish! My word, but I had no idea you were such a flirt."

He couldn't stop himself from smiling without pretense. He enjoyed her company; he had from the moment she'd begun to regain her strength and charmed him with stories of her youth. A pampered daughter of the aristocracy who had married a man who delivered harsh lessons that destroyed her naivety but not her spirit. "Only when it comes to you."

"I find that difficult to believe. I suspect all of Victoria's ladies-in-waiting are stumbling over themselves to get your attention."

"Your suspicions are without foundation. I fear my flirtation skills are a trifle rusty. I've not had much time for the ladies since I began serving Victoria." The women for whom he'd had time were the sort who required nothing beyond coins.

She wrapped her hand around the crook of his elbow. "Shall we go into dinner then?"

"I'm famished." He stopped short of saying he was famished for her. His true seduction would come after dinner because he wanted to ensure that he stayed in the residence throughout the night as close to her as possible. While he felt a niggling of guilt at the role he was about the play, he assuaged it by reminding himself that he was doing it to protect her.

Jack had sent a couple of his minions over to watch the residence, and Swindler had made arrangements for a few extra bobbies to patrol the streets, but Graves felt a need to take his own precautions to ensure that if her blasted husband was around, he would be near enough to deal with him—preferably with her being none the wiser.

He had Claybourne's grandfather to thank for the manners he brought to the table with him. When the old gent had discovered his grandson was a child of the rookeries, he'd not only taken him in but taken in his friends as well. It was then that Graves had learned the comforts of a clean bed, a bath, clothes that fit properly. He never took any of his comforts for granted.

He settled Winnie into her chair and then sat in the one opposite her. He was grateful they were being served in the smaller dining room and that the table was a modest one that would sit only six. The family dining room.

White wine was poured and the first course was served: a soup that was more broth than substance, but he couldn't fault its flavor.

"I feared you might not survive your encounter with Catherine," he said, striving to keep his voice level so it didn't reveal his curiosity regarding what might have been said after he left. Catherine might have cautioned her not to become involved with him, which would mean he'd have to work all the harder at seduction.

"She warned me away from you."

"I'm not surprised. You see me as a man of goodness, but I assure you I am more scoundrel than saint. I became a physician because I had much to atone for."

"Such as?"

"Nothing a lady needs to hear about, especially over dinner."

Watching as she lifted the spoon to her lips, he found himself envious of a damned eating utensil. When she returned it to the bowl, she lifted her gaze to his, studied him for a moment. He wondered if she were able to see beneath the surface, to the part of him that he shared with no one.

"I know you grew up on the streets," she said. "What was it like?"

While she'd been recovering, she hadn't asked about his youth. He rather wished she hadn't asked now. "Dirty. Harsh. But within Feagan's den there was a sense of camaraderie."

"Who is Feagan?"

"The kidsman who corralled us, taught us to steal and pilfer without getting caught."

"What of your parents?"

He took a sip of his wine. "My mother washed clothes. What I remember most about her was how rough and raw her hands always looked." How rough they felt when they grazed against his skin when she was in a rage and he served as the object upon which she could vent her anger. It was like being slapped with sandpaper. "My father earned his living digging graves in various cemeteries and pauper's fields. And at night, he'd return to rob the graves. When I was big enough to hold a trowel, he took me with him."

The bowl was removed and a plate of mutton was set before them but she hardly seemed to notice. "Weren't you frightened, going into the graveyards at night?"

"What was there to dread?"

"The spirits of the dead. Don't you believe they linger?"

As she had mentioned being haunted before, he didn't laugh. "To haunt us?"

"Yes, quite."

Pondering his answer, he took a bite of the tasty mutton. She was so earnest. Who was he to dissuade her from her beliefs? "I will admit that I have encountered phenomenon that is difficult to explain: A glow in the fog, a howling when there is no wind. And on occasion, the hairs on the back of my neck would rise. Sometimes I felt that I was being watched, but I assumed it was other grave robbers who were disappointed we beat them to the treasures."

She glanced around and he knew she wanted to say more, perhaps even mention the strange occurrences she'd experienced of late, but she was hesitant to appear foolish in front of the servants, even if they weren't supposed to be listening.

"So you've never actually seen a spirit wandering around the graves?" Before he could answer, her eyes widened. "Is that why your surname is Graves?"

He couldn't help but smile. She looked as though she'd

solved a difficult problem. "When Feagan took in a child, he always made him or her change their name. For most of us there is no record of our birth, no record of our existence. Unlike with the aristocracy where births and deaths are recorded steadfastly, in the rookeries names are changed on a whim or when someone is caught committing a crime."

"It never occurred to me that one could go about changing his name so easily."

"I suspect even some of your servants aren't presently living under the name with which they were born." He didn't fail to notice how one of the footmen shifted his stance. He'd have to check the man out. Probably wouldn't hurt to have Swindler investigate them all. He'd much rather discover it was one of them instead of Avendale sneaking about.

"So why Graves?" she asked as another dish was set before them.

"An homage to my father, to his work. He was a large man, silent as the grave, which seemed appropriate considering his occupation. Never complained, never had an unkind word. 'Lot of unpleasant tasks need doing,' he once told me. 'So it's best to just do them so you can move on to the pleasant ones.'"

"How did he die?"

"Don't know that he did. He simply disappeared one night. After he sold my mother's remains to a teaching hospital." As a look of horror crossed her face, he downed his wine, signaled for more. This time he was brought red.

"That's awful," she said, brushing away the next plate before it could be placed before her.

"I've ruined your appetite. Perhaps we should discuss the weather. It's going to rain tonight, I predict."

"I don't want to discuss the rain. Were you there? Did you see what he did with your mother?"

He took a healthy swallow of the wine, wishing for something a bit stronger. He'd not thought of his youth in years. "I was with him. I found no fault with his decision. We were in need of coins, but more than that, Winnie, those training to become doctors needed to be able to study more than books. My mum was quite unpleasant in life, but in death, I believe, she became an instrument of education that allowed others to save lives."

"I suppose that's one way to think of it."

"It's the only way to think of it."

"We are so morbidly fascinated with death. You've dealt with it all your life in one manner or another. You don't fear it?"

He slowly shook his head. "No."

"Do you fear anything?"

You discovering the truth. Not that he could admit to that.

"That it'll rain before I can take you on a turn about the garden."

She laughed the sweet tinkling sound that reminded him of tiny crystal bells ringing on Christmas morning. "I'm serious."

"As am I." Shoving back his chair, he stood, walked over to her, and pulled out her chair. Leaning low, he said in a quiet, seductive voice, "Come on, Winnie. It's dark out. Lovely things happen in the dark."

With a twinkle in her eyes, she peered up at him and whispered, "But we've yet to have dessert."

"I have my heart set on tasting something sweeter than anything that can be prepared in the kitchen."

Rising, she placed her hand on his forearm. "A walk about the garden sounds just the thing."

Unfortunately as they stepped out onto the covered terrace, they discovered a soft rain falling, so quietly as to create little more than a constant drone rather than a harsh pattering of drops.

"We're too late," she said.

"We're never too late." He walked to the edge of the terrace, just short of being touched by the falling droplets. "I find the rain soothing."

He felt her shiver. Stepping behind her, he wrapped his arms around her and drew her in close.

"I feared it when I was a child," she said quietly. "When the lightning rent the sky in two and thunder boomed so loud that it shook the ground, the servants would rush through the house turning all the mirrors around. It was my mother's edict. She said when she was a child a bolt of lightning zigzagged through her parents' house, using the mirrors to propel itself along. Do you think that's possible?"

"I think anything's possible." Lowering his head, he kissed the nape of her neck, where jasmine behind her ear overpowered the scent of rain. He wondered where else she may have applied the fragrance. He kissed the other side. "Are your parents alive now?"

"No, it's only Whit and I. He thought it was such an adventure when we spent time in your residence."

"He's a good lad. We should take him to the park one afternoon." He trailed his mouth from one shoulder to the other, relishing her sigh.

"He went to the zoological gardens today. He's drawing

me pictures of the animals he saw." Her voice sounded faint, faraway as though she were floating into oblivion.

"I should like to see them."

"I'll show you when he's finished."

He nipped at her ear before slowing turning her around. Lifting her hand, she rubbed the bridge of her nose. He wrapped his hand around her wrist. "Don't," he said gently. "Don't cover your nose."

"It's unsightly."

"Nothing, absolutely nothing about you is unsightly."

She released a self-conscious laugh. "Sometimes I forget that you've seen all of me."

"I looked upon you as a physician—which is a cold and impersonal observation. When I look upon you as a man, it will be very much like seeing you for the first time."

She gave the tiniest mewl as though it had not occurred to her before that what he'd implied would most certainly happen. Sometimes he forgot that she was a lady first, a woman second. That she wasn't accustomed to traveling the path he wanted to travel.

Still, he brought her in close and took her mouth, while the rain cooled and scented the air. Her tongue parried with his, her hands combed through his hair, her sighs mingled with his moans. Sweet, so gloriously sweet. He could have—

"Excuse me, Your Grace."

She jerked back as though the butler had taken a lash to her. "Yes, Thatcher, what is it?"

"A missive from the queen for Dr. Graves."

Graves held out his hand, and Thatcher extended the silver salver. He took the letter bearing the royal crest, opened it, and walked over to the doorway where enough light spilled out so he could read the words.

"What is it?" Winnie asked, coming to stand beside him.

"I'm being summoned." With an apologetic sigh, he said, "I must go."

"Of course you must."

He cradled her face. "Thank you for dinner. I can't remember when I've enjoyed a night more."

"If it's not too late when you're finished, perhaps you could come back to enjoy your after-dinner port. I'll feel like a horrible hostess otherwise."

He grinned. "We can't have that. But I have no idea how long it'll take."

She glanced back over her shoulder. "Thatcher, give the doctor a key to the residence before he leaves."

"Winnie—" Graves began. They would be opening a door they would be unlikely to close.

She nodded, somewhat jerkily. "I want you to have a key. If I'm asleep, you can awaken me and I'll get the port for you."

If he were to awaken her, it wouldn't be for bloody port, not that he was going to confess to that with the butler standing there. Leaning in, he kissed her gently. "I'll return when I can. I should warn you that it could be days."

"I'll be waiting."

Don't be, he almost told her. No good would come of it.

With the flame in the lamp turned low, Winnie lay in her bed, listening as the rain beat against the pane. It was coming down with more force now, and she thought of William traveling through it, dashing from the carriage to her door, his hair damp when he came to her.

It was after midnight. She'd waited up as long as she could, but she was tired now, so tired. She'd taken great pains to prepare for bed. Her nightdress was satin. It revealed very little. The matching wrap was resting at the foot of the bed, so she could snatch it up quickly when William arrived. Her maid had brushed her hair a hundred times before braiding it. She'd applied a dab of perfume behind her ears, just a small dab, because he seemed to enjoy kissing her neck.

She could hardly fathom that she'd given him a key to the residence, that she was considering allowing him into her bed. But she loved the way he made her feel: precious, treasured. They'd not spoken of love or a future, but it hardly mattered. She just needed something to erase the memories of what happened the last time a man had taken her in this bed. She squeezed her eyes shut. No, not this bed. She'd had that one carted away, had purchased a new one to replace it. Only she had ever slept in it. Not entirely true. Her lips curled up. Whit had joined her a time or two when he had a bad dream. But he was older now, beginning to show a preference for not being coddled by his mother.

Her eyelids began growing heavy. William would return when he could, and she was anticipating it as she'd not anticipated anything in a good long while. He would open the door, slip beneath the sheets, take her into his arms—

The silk slid over her body as his hands caressed her, the silk no barrier to the heat of his touch. He nuzzled her neck. "I returned as soon as I could."

She didn't want words, didn't need them. All she wanted were the marvelous sensations that he seemed able to elicit with so little effort. She was floating on a cloud of pleasure, his hands and mouth taking her to places where she'd never traveled. Heat scorched her, inside and out. She wanted to touch him, to feel his skin, but she seemed unable to grasp anything of substance. He was like shadows, weaving around her—

She inhaled his sandalwood scent, but her lungs froze, her nose stung. Not sandalwood. Caraway. Cloying. Suffocating.

His hands closed around her throat. She couldn't breathe. He was weighing her down, taking her into the depths of hell. She fought, she kicked, she screamed a silent scream that was somehow more terrifying. She was going to die! He was going to—

Winnie awoke with a jolt, breathing heavily, her body trembling. She scrambled back until she was sitting against the headboard. Most of the room was ensconced in wavering shadows that danced around the corners and over the ceiling. The lamp was no longer burning, but there was a fire in the hearth. She didn't remember there being a fire when she went to sleep.

The room was chilled and damp. The windows were open, the draperies pulled aside, and the curtains of lighter fabric blowing in the breeze as rain pattered against the floor. Had William returned and opened them? Then where was he?

And why was the caraway scent stronger now? She was trembling, her silk nightdress clinging to her dampened skin. She had to get hold of herself. Some warm milk, some warm milk would help.

She reached for the lamp to relight it and froze.

There, resting on the corner of the bedside table were

two rings—ducal rings—that had belonged to her husband. She'd left them in a safe at the ancestral estate, to be given to Whit when he was older and his fingers large enough to accommodate them.

So how the devil had they ended up there?

CHAPTER FIVE

With the rain pelting his hat and coat, Graves stood outside Winnie's residence. It was half past four in the morning. She was no doubt asleep by now. If he unlocked that door, walked into her residence, into her bedchamber, everything would change. There would be no going back.

As much as he wanted her, he didn't want her under these circumstances. He hadn't expected his actions toward her to result in her welcoming him so quickly and swiftly. While his feelings for her might be honest, his reasons for pursuing her at the moment were not.

He should turn about and go home. But he was the only one with the ability to stay near enough to her to protect them all. Staying close to her would certainly prove no hardship—at least not until she was no longer content with only the small part he would offer.

Do no harm. That was the mantra of his profession, but in her case he had failed to heed it, which was why he was now standing in the blasted rain arguing with himself. He didn't have to wake her. He could just sit in a chair and watch her.

That seemed the way to go. To torment himself further by being near enough to touch her, but refraining. That would definitely qualify him for sainthood.

He marched up the steps, slipped the key into the lock, let himself in, and locked the door behind him. Within the foyer, all was silent, hushed. A lamp had been left to burn on a table. He had far too many nights where lamps were left to burn for him as he sat vigil, striving to ward off death, but it snuck by him when it was good and ready. Alone in his residence, he mourned the loss of every patient while he analyzed every step of the treatment, striving to understand why sometimes things worked and sometimes they didn't. There was always more to learn, so much more to learn.

If he didn't go up those grand sweeping stairs, if they were correct about the danger, if something happened to her, he would analyze this night until the what-ifs drove him mad.

Leaving his damp hat and coat on a rack in the foyer, he grabbed the lamp and started up the stairs. He fought to tamp down the anticipation building with each step. He was only going to watch her sleep, nothing more. But he could certainly take pleasure in that.

Three years before, he'd been awoken in the dead of night to come here. Outside her door, he came to a stop as the images assailed him: her battered face, her badly beaten body. He'd never seen anyone covered in so many bruises, and he'd dealt with survivors of a train wreck. He flattened his palm against the door. Unlike Claybourne and Jack, he'd never had a penchant for violence, but that night, he thought if her husband had stepped into the room, he might have very well killed him. That a man could willingly inflict so much harm on another human being, on a woman, on his wife—Graves was neither innocent nor naive but sometimes he did not understand the minds of men.

Quietly he opened the door. A weak fire struggling to remain relevant chased shadows around the room. His heart lurched at the sight of the rumpled, but empty bed. Quickly he stepped farther into the room. Rain was coming in through the open windows, pooling on the floor. Then he spotted her huddled in a corner, shivering uncontrollably. He rushed across the room and crouched before her. "Winnie, sweetheart?"

She lifted a dazed gaze to his.

Cautiously he cradled her face in his palm. "Did you have a bad dream?"

Jerkily she shook her head and lifted a shaking hand, pointing with one finger. "I don't . . . know . . . how they got here."

Twisting around, he studied the bed where she indicated. "What precisely?"

"On the table."

Unfolding his body, he strode over to the bedside table. His gut clenched as he picked up the two rings. He knew them well. He'd placed them on a pauper's fingers. Inwardly, he cursed harshly, but outwardly he gave no sign of his alarm or trepidation. He halfway hoped the blighter was still in the residence. If they crossed paths, Graves would be digging a grave before the night was out.

But when he turned back to Winnie, he knew he couldn't leave her, not like this. Nor could he tell her the truth of it. At that moment she was all that mattered. After slipping the rings into his trousers' pocket, he walked back over to her. "It's going to be all right."

Lifting her in his arms, he carried her over to the bed, gently laid her down, and drew the covers over her. "Would you like me to close the windows?"

She nodded, and he marched over to them, closing one and then the other. He took a moment to peer through them. *Are you out there, you bastard?*

With quickness, he drew the draperies closed. Aware of her gaze following him, he went into the bathing room, snatched up some linens, and returned to spread them over the floor beneath the windows so they could soak up the water.

As he neared the bed, he tore off his jacket, waistcoat, and cravat and tossed them on a nearby chair. After pulling off his shoes, he sat on the edge of the bed. "Winnie, you appear to be in shock. You need to be warmed. I'm going to slip beneath the covers and hold you. That's all, just hold you. All right?"

Her eyes wide and circular, she nodded. "I'm going mad."

"No, sweetheart, there's an explanation for all this," he murmured as he worked his way between the sheets and drew her near, briskly rubbing his hands up and down her back, striving to generate enough heat to stop her trembling. Her teeth were chattering. He feared he might have to wake the servants to have a warm bath prepared for her. Although he suspected she wouldn't want the servants to see her like this. "Can you tell me what happened?"

Snuggling up against him, she burrowed her nose into the crook of his shoulder. "I was dreaming, and suddenly I began to feel as though a great weight was pressing on me and I was suffocating. I could smell Avendale as though he were wafting through the room. I don't recall opening the windows or building the fire. Or the rings. How did they come to be here? They were locked up safe at the family estate. Could I be doing these things in my sleep?"

At least she'd stopped trembling, he was grateful for that. He slowed his hands into a gentle caress. "It's possible I suppose. I once had a patient who would wake up in the middle of the night to find himself standing in the stables with no recollection of how he came to be there."

She tilted her head up to hold his gaze. "Truly?"

He gave her a comforting smile. "Truly. He also was stark naked. Apparently, he removed his nightclothes before he began his trek."

She released a little huff that was almost a laugh. "Were you able to cure him?"

"No, I couldn't determine the cause. It wasn't physical and there's a good deal I don't know about the mind."

"Do I belong in Bedlam, do you think?"

"No, absolutely not," he said with conviction.

She nestled her face back against his chest. "Is everything all right with the queen?"

"Yes. She ate something that upset her digestion."

"She's fortunate to have you."

He pressed a kiss to the top of her head. "Go to sleep now. I'll hold the monsters and nightmares at bay."

"Yes, all right."

He was acutely aware of her relaxing against him, her breathing slowing.

"I've never slept with a man in my bed before," she said in a low voice, as though she feared disturbing him. "I rather like it. Avendale always left right afterward."

Naturally. The man didn't appreciate what he once possessed. "I don't."

"I suspected that about you." He thought he could feel a blush warming her skin beneath his hands. "You're always so kind."

Her words were like a lash to his heart. If he were kind he would tell her everything right now and end her torment, only others were involved, those with whom he'd grown up, those who had saved his neck on more than one occasion. Claybourne especially. If not for him, Graves would no doubt still be on the streets or worse, dead. "Try to sleep."

He was acutely aware of the length of her body pressed against his. One of her legs was wedged between his and he fought not to consider that her leg was bare which meant that her gown was hiked up. How far up, he couldn't tell. At his side, her hand flinched, unfurled. Her breathing went soft, softer.

He kept his arms around her, holding her close, hoping that with his presence he could hold her fears at bay.

Winnie awoke to find William raised up on an elbow, watching her. The fire had long since gone out. With the draperies drawn, no sunlight was entering the room. The only light came from the soft glow of the lamp that he'd brought into the room with him the night before.

She wasn't yet ready to speak, to disturb his study of

her, especially as she wanted to take a few moments to enjoy the sight of him. Although his hair was blond, he had the longest, blackest eyelashes she'd ever seen. Unlike hers, his nose was straight and perfect, narrow, patrician. His chin was narrow, sharp, with the tiniest dent in the center of it. His cheekbones were high, hollowed. The bristles along his jaw were darker than she'd expected them to be. She had an insane thought that she would very much like to shave him, feel and hear the scrape of the razor over his skin.

She thought of doing things with him that she never thought of doing with Avendale. William appealed to her in ways that Avendale never had. She had cared for Avendale, had believed when she accepted his offer of marriage that she loved him, but now she could not help but wonder if perhaps she had been too young to truly recognize love, if perhaps she had simply been in love with the notion of love, or perhaps marriage. It was what girls of her station strived to accomplish: a good marriage. Or maybe he had managed to beat out her affections toward him until no remnants of her original feelings for him remained, and so she could no longer remember exactly how she had felt toward him.

"Did you sleep?" she asked William.

"I promised to keep watch," he said with a small smile and a hoarse voice that stirred something deep inside her. It implied secret trysts. "Besides, I don't need much sleep, and I rarely go an entire night without someone knocking on my door."

"I can't help but feel I've become quite the nuisance."

"You haven't. I wouldn't be here if I didn't want to be." He tucked his finger beneath her chin and stroked her cheek with his thumb. "Are you feeling a bit more settled?"

"Somewhat. I'm quite embarrassed with the spectacle I made of myself last night."

"You have nothing for which to be embarrassed. A nightmare can be upsetting enough without the strange occurrences you're experiencing."

"I just don't understand what's happening."

"I think someone is striving to drive you mad."

"But who and for what purpose?"

Turning his attention to the braid draped over her shoulder, he brushed his fingers through the loose strands at the end, seemingly mesmerized by the movements. "That I don't know, but I'm wondering if it wouldn't be wiser for you and your son to move into my residence." He shifted his solemn gaze back to hers. "Just for a few days."

She had felt so welcomed in his home, so at ease. It was there that she had come to realize the horror that her life had truly become. As she gained her strength, he allowed her to determine the menu for the meals. He never found fault with her selections. He never criticized if she spent her mornings reading or composing letters. For the first time in her life, the hours of the day became hers to do with as she pleased. He had given her glimpses of a life that didn't encompass fear.

"I truly, truly appreciate the offer, but I'll not be chased out of my own home. I don't think Whit is in any danger. His governess hasn't reported any strange goings on. All that is happening just seems directed at me. Perhaps I do have a disgruntled servant. I'll speak with Thatcher, have him watch them a bit more closely."

"I admire your resolve." He traced the curve of her cheek. "But I don't think you've quite recovered from last night's misadventure. I have a morning ritual that I don't always get to indulge in but I think it would be just the thing to chase the last of the shadows from your eyes."

He was looking at her so intently, as though he were memorizing every line and curve of her features, every bump and every scar. His intensity had all sorts of notions racing through her mind, notions no proper lady should entertain. Morning rituals that included kissing and touching, hands on her thighs, her stomach, her breasts. She wasn't certain she was quite ready for that, but she heard herself asking, "What sort of ritual?"

"Rowing."

She blinked in surprise. Was that what the lower classes called it? She supposed she could see that, but not quite. And he might have once been ensconced among the dregs of society, but he had risen above that to a respected—and, in her mind at least—an exalted position. Surely he no longer used such crude references. She licked her lips. "What exactly does it entail?"

"A boat, oars, the Thames."

"Oh, you mean actual rowing?"

With a grin, he skimmed his finger along the bridge of her nose. "What did you think I was alluding to?"

She was going to embarrass herself by admitting the truth. "Exactly what you said." She was intrigued. "You truly go rowing in the morning?"

"Whenever I can before breakfast."

Glancing over at the clock, she realized it was much earlier than she thought. "It must still be dark out."

"It won't be by the time we get there. Come with me. I think you'll find it's a refreshing way to begin the day."

She thought doing anything with him would be a lovely way to start the day. "Yes, all right."

CHAPTER SIX

With her pelisse folded closely around her, Winnie sat in the rowboat and watched in fascination as William worked the oars in a steady rhythm that caused the boat to glide smoothly over the water. She had looked in on Whit before she left, and he'd been sleeping soundly. On Winnie's orders the day before, the governess had left the door to her apartments open so she could hear Whit if anything was amiss. Not that anything seemed to be. The fragrance of caraway seeds had faded, and she was questioning whether or not it had ever been there.

Forcing the worries from her mind, she concentrated on enjoying her outing. Wisps of light fog along the bank were beginning to burn off as the sky lightened from black to gray. The scent of last night's rain was still heavy on the air.

Once she was settled in the boat, William removed his jacket and rolled up his sleeves, took the oars in hand, and set off. No leisurely rowing. His forearms revealed corded muscles, and she understood now the breadth of his shoulders, the firmness of his chest.

"Whatever possessed you to take up this sport?" she asked.

"One of Victoria's advisors begins his day in a similar manner, and mentioned it to me. I've discovered an hour of strenuous activity clears my mind of its cobwebs. Sometimes, when I'm faced with a medical problem or dilemma, I find the solution will often come to me when I'm out here. I become lost in the exertion and it frees up my mind."

He stopped rowing, and they coasted to a stop. She became aware of the quiet and the solitude, absolute solitude as she'd never experienced it.

Sliding from the bench, he sat with his back to it and extended a hand to her. "Come here, sit with your back to me. Just move carefully so you don't tip us over."

The boat wobbled as she very slowly eased down and turned so she was nestled between his legs, her back pressed to his chest. He slid his arms around her, holding her near, and the heat of his body seeped through the layers of her clothes to create marvelous radiating warmth.

"Watch the sky," he said in a low voice near her ear.

Leaning against him, tilting her head back slightly, she was acutely aware of his cheek resting against hers. Above the trees lining the banks, the sky was deep orange and pink with dark blue swirling through it. The clouds seemed luminescent.

"I don't think I've ever seen a sunrise," she whispered with reverence.

"It's my understanding that most ladies stay abed until late morning."

"It does seem to be our habit. Oh, it's beautiful, isn't it? Magnificent."

They gazed in silence for several long moments. She relished his nearness, his holding her. She'd never been held simply for the pleasure of being held. There was comfort in it, an easing of loneliness without words. It was so peaceful. She was glad that William had stopped. Her soul needed these moments.

"It rather fills me with wonder," she told him. "It's a lovely way to begin the day. Have you always enjoyed the sunrise?"

"When I was on my own, before I crossed paths with Feagan, I was a mudlark."

While she had only seen them from afar, she knew the term was applied to children who scrounged through the muddy banks of the Thames searching for washed up items to sell. It seemed a rather bleak existence. But she heard no play for sympathy in his voice. He spoke of his past as though it were truly in his past, as though it no longer had any influence on his life, and she wondered how he had achieved that end. She suspected that Avendale and his treatment of her would always manage to have some hold over her.

"I would go out while it was still dark," he continued, "hoping to beat the other children to the prize collections for the day. The sky would begin to lighten, the fog would dissipate, and the sun would start to make its presence known. I would look up and think, 'How can there be such beauty up there, when everything down here is so gray?' It gave me hope that I would find something better someday."

"Have you?"

"I have no right to complain when I deal with the sick and infirmed, and am constantly reminded that I have a good deal for which to be thankful." He nuzzled her neck. "But sometimes, I do find myself wishing for more."

Turning her slightly, he took her mouth, his tongue delving deeply, his hand cradling the back of her head, his arm bracing her spine as he leaned her over. Even knowing that he held her secure, that he wouldn't let her fall, she clutched at his shirt, knotting her fingers around the cloth. In the distance, she was aware of the day beginning for many, the rattle of carriage wheels, the yells of those doing business out in the open, yet she gave no thought to the fact that someone might see her in this precarious position. She should mind that he brazenly kissed her out here where all the world could see, but no one she knew would be about. Ladies and most gents were still abed. They missed the sunrise, they missed the peace and quiet of the morning starting anew.

They missed the passion that ignited so quickly and fiercely between her and William.

She wondered if he brought her here because he'd known where things might end up if he kissed her in her bedchamber, in her bed. Nothing beyond a kiss would happen in this small boat that rocked on the Thames, nothing would happen in the open where curious eyes could take note of improper behavior.

Even with her pelisse wrapped around her, she'd been quite cool earlier, but now she was burning with a fever that raged only for him, for his touch, his nearness. His kiss seemed to encompass more than her lips. She felt it through her entire quivering body. Lovely warmth, and flaming passion. His mouth was greedily devouring hers, but she had no desire for him to stop. She was coming to life, her nerve endings rejoicing with the sensations he so easily awakened.

Resting her palm against his jaw, she took delight in the

bristles. He hadn't taken the time to tidy up before bringing her out here, and it added an additional element of improperness to what they were doing. She, who had strived so hard to do everything that was proper, was suddenly being carried along on a stream of wickedness.

Dragging his mouth from hers, he dipped it into the curve of her neck, and she thought surely he would leave a mark that everyone would see. She could hardly bring herself to care.

"Winnie," he rasped, his breathing as harsh and heavy as hers.

What else he might have said was lost as the soft slap of oars on water had them both drawing back. With a quick salute a man rowed by them. No one she recognized, so it was unlikely that her reputation would be torn to tatters.

With care, William eased her upright. In his eyes, she saw desire smoldering. It was a heady rush to realize how much he wanted her. Even more astonishing to her was the realization that she desperately yearned for him, that she didn't fear what might pass between them, but rather found herself anticipating it.

Quite suddenly, without warning, the hairs on the back of her neck began to prickle, and she had the overwhelming sense of being watched, of someone discerning the direction of her thoughts. Jerking her head around, she scoured the banks.

"What is it?" he asked.

A shiver raced through her. "Someone's watching."

He looked at the trees and brush lining the water's edge. "The man who just rowed by us, perhaps."

"No, this feels almost sinister."

"Winnie, there's no one about."

He's hiding, she wanted to tell him. He means us harm, but she would sound truly mad. She couldn't see anyone, and who would want to hurt her? Avendale was the only one who ever had. Everyone else treated her kindly. She released a self-conscious laugh. "I'm sorry, I'm ruining our lovely morning."

"You don't need to apologize, and you're not ruining anything." He studied her with concern that made her feel silly for raising an alarm. She had absolutely no reason to feel threatened and yet she did. It was almost as though Avendale's gaze was boring a hole through her back. He'd had such an intense stare that she'd been able to feel it at the most crowded of balls, no matter where he was in the room.

"I think perhaps remnants of last night are lingering," he said, taking strands of her hair that the wind had tugged free of the braid and tucking them behind her ear. How could such a simple act of putting her back together feel so remarkably intimate, set her back to rights in so many ways? All her fears dissipated as gently as the fog.

"Yes, I think you're right. I thought I was over the fright from last night."

"How would you like to row us back?" he asked.

"I don't believe I'd have the strength."

"I'm relatively certain you're stronger than you realize. I'll sit behind you and guide you until you have the hang of it." Pushing himself up, careful not to rock the boat overmuch, he sat on the bench and then assisted her into position, so she was sitting between his thighs. When she took hold of the oars, he folded his hands over hers. "You can't make any mistakes here."

His faith in her caused her chest to tighten. She'd once become accustomed to not being able to do anything correctly. It was quite liberating to know William was not awaiting an opportunity to scold her.

"Whenever you're ready," he said, and she thought she'd never been more ready to take on a task.

As she moved the oars, she was quite aware of his strength serving to guide her. She felt the muscles of his powerful chest tightening and loosening against her back, the ropy muscles of his arms bunching and undulating with his movements. They moved in tandem, rocking forward, leaning back, working together to skim over the water. She thought anything he did with her would mirror this togetherness, this partnership. She imagined what a fortunate woman his wife would be.

"Why have you never married?" she asked.

"I fear it would take a very special woman to be content with the life I can offer her, leaving her bed at all hours, arriving for dinner after the food has cooled, or having the meal interrupted when she is in the midst of telling me about her day. My schedule is seldom governed by the clock."

"That sounds rather like something you would say at social affairs when meddling mothers are trying to foist their daughters off on you."

His low chuckle tickled her soul. "Quite right."

While she considered questioning him further, she decided to let it pass. His reasons were obviously personal or he would have shared them without her having to pull the answer from him. If she could characterize their relationship at all, she would do so using the term "completely honest." He'd never lied to her, never deceived her. She could be herself with him without fear of judgment, and she accepted him as he was. It was quite freeing, to have that amount of trust with someone.

Oh, she certainly trusted Catherine, but her trust of William was more complete, more firm. It was the bedrock upon which a foundation of something deeper could be built. He gave her confidence in herself that had been sorely lacking before. He allowed her to trust herself.

Her muscles began to burn with the relentless rowing, but she took satisfaction in it. Then she realized that his hands were no longer folded over hers, but merely resting atop them, that he was moving with her but his muscles weren't knotting with effort.

"I'm doing this on my own, aren't I?" she asked.

"I was wondering when you might notice."

"You make me believe I can do anything, that I truly have nothing to fear."

"You can do anything," he said quietly. "I truly believe that."

They were nearing their destination, the small dock where boats were stored and rented.

"I'll guide us in," he said. "It can get tricky."

As much as she didn't want to, she accepted the wisdom of his words. She was still a novice, but she felt invincible. While he took over the oars, she folded her hands in her lap.

"I need to face my demons," she said succinctly. "I think all these strange occurrences that have been happening are tied in with Avendale."

He stilled, the oars out of the water, droplets dripping into the Thames. "Why would you think that?"

"Because I never truly let him go. I've allowed him to maintain a hold over me. If I'm not going mad, then something has to be moving those objects around, causing all those unexplainable things to be happening. I think his spirit might be haunting me. Even out here, the strange sensation I had of being watched, I think I can attribute it to him."

"You think he's visiting you along the lines of Marley's ghost?"

She didn't blame him for the skepticism. It sounded rather ludicrous to her, but she could think of no other explanation. Easing over to the other bench, she faced him. "I have an old aunt who swears she's communed with her dead husband. The medium she used—I believe her name was Mrs. Ponsby—was able to serve as a vessel so my aunt could ask her husband where he had hidden her jewels. Before he died, he'd gone quite off his rocker, hiding all sorts of things. He thought everyone was trying to steal from him. Anyway, through Mrs. Ponsby, he told my aunt where in the garden she'd find her jewels. They were exactly where they were supposed to be. I think Mrs. Ponsby could assist me in speaking with Avendale. I want him to know that I won't put up with this nonsense. He must move on."

"Winnie, I fear it'll be a waste of your coin."

"It's my coin to waste. But after my aunt's experience, I'm quite confident in the medium's ability to speak with the dead. I don't know why I didn't think of calling on her before. It's as you said earlier, being out here frees up the mind to all sorts of possibilities. If I can make him see that I'm not the woman I was, that he can't push me around, that I don't frighten as easily, perhaps he'll let me be. That's the thing of it. He took joy from my cowering. I know that I reacted rather badly last night, but that's because I thought I was going mad. If it's Avendale, then I need to have a word with him."

"I just don't think you'll accomplish anything." With a final dip and push of the oars, he had the boat gliding alongside the deck.

"I think it's worth a try. If you'd rather not be there—"

"I'll be there."

"She plans to have a medium connect her with Avendale's spirit," Graves said to the group gathered in Claybourne's library. Claybourne, Catherine, Frannie, Swindler, and Jack. It was early afternoon. He didn't like talking about Winnie's plans behind her back, but he owed these people, although he was beginning to feel as though he was giving them his soul.

He hadn't wanted to leave Winnie but he'd needed to see to some patients, and as his first was the queen herself, he couldn't very well be late to that appointment. Victoria seemed to have recovered from her bout of illness. He wished taking care of Winnie's situation would prove to be as easy.

"I'll convince her that no good will come of it," Catherine said.

"Let her do it," Jack said. "Where's the harm? The medium will raise the table a bit with her knees, make knocking sounds on her chair, hum for a spell, and then pretend to be possessed by a spirit. The duchess will believe she's spoken to her dead husband, and won't even begin to consider that he isn't dead at all."

"He's right," Frannie said. "It will only serve to reinforce our ruse."

Graves wasn't convinced. "And if this medium doesn't contact her husband?"

"She will," Swindler said. "They're all charlatans. I've arrested several. Attended the séances to gather the information to prove that they were not contacting the dead as claimed, but swindling people out of money. While I'm opposed to their methods, I agree that in this case they serve our purpose."

Graves didn't feel comfortable with it. "What we did three years ago was necessary. What we're doing now, to protect ourselves, doesn't sit well with me."

"Think you'll feel more comfortable when you're dancing in the wind?" Jack asked. "He's a bloody duke. You're a commoner."

"He's physician to the queen," Claybourne pointed out.

"Knowing how she and Albert are striving to raise the standard of behavior among her subjects," Jack said, "do you think she's going to be open to looking the other way?"

Silence greeted that proclamation as they all knew that Victoria had high moral values. Within her court, she was known for dismissing servants for the slightest of infractions.

"We might want to consider another possibility," Swindler said, his sharp gaze homing in on Graves. "That the duchess is the one instigating a ruse."

"Why the devil would she do that?" Graves asked.

"To gain your attention. Have you seen any evidence that what she claims is happening is in fact happening? She's always telling you things after the fact."

While he thought it highly unlikely, he couldn't discount the question entirely. She had mentioned the necklace disappearing, then showed up at his door with it. She knew he would be returning to the residence last night. She could have arranged the rings, then sat in the corner awaiting his arrival. But he thought of her haunted eyes, her chills, her trembling. "I've no doubt she's telling me the truth."

"I agree with Bill's assessment," Catherine said. "Winnie doesn't have a conniving bone in her body. I'll visit her this afternoon. She's certain to invite me to attend her séance, and Claybourne and I cat at least be on hand to reinforce the notion that Avendale is dead."

"I'll be there as well tonight," Graves told her.

"Well then I don't see that anything can go wrong," Jack said.

Winnie had chosen the duke's library for the séance. He'd spent a good deal of his life there, overseeing the management of his estates. In spite of its size, which allowed for four large sitting areas, this room seemed to have absorbed his strong scent. The dark heavy furniture reminded her so much of the bold and brazen man he'd been.

"Why would anyone require a desk that large?" she asked William, while the servants rearranged one of the sitting areas at the behest of Mrs. Ponsby, who was quite renowned for her ability to commune with the dead.

"It made him feel important," William responded to her question.

"And I hate the gargoyles," she said. The hideous stone

creatures sat on either side of the fireplace grate. "He took them from a dilapidated church, or so he said. Still, it seemed rather sacrilegious. To be quite honest, there is nothing in this room that I like, except for the books. I suppose I should redo it." Where there weren't shelves, there were paintings of battles and people lying about bloodied. They always gave her chills, which was another reason she thought this room would serve them well. It seemed to celebrate death and suffering.

"Are you sure about this, Winnie?" Catherine asked. In the late afternoon, she'd stopped by for a spot of tea, and Winnie had taken the opportunity to invite her and Claybourne to join her that evening for the séance.

"Yes, I'm sure. He made my life quite miserable while he was alive. I shan't have him doing it while he's dead." She squeezed William's arm. "As you weren't afraid of the dead when you were a lad, I see no reason that I should be as a grown woman."

"I'm just not certain that you're going to speak with him as clearly as you seem to think you will," William said. "Calling out to the dead has not been proven to be scientifically possible."

"Have you ever had a patient who you were certain was going to die, based upon your knowledge of the human body and medicine, but he recovered from his illness or wounds?"

"Yes. You."

She was taken aback by his answer although she knew she shouldn't have been. That dreadful night, she'd been certain she would die, but she just hadn't been able to succumb and leave Whit. "There are some things that simply can't be explained," she said softly. "Mrs. Ponsby says it's more likely to work if everyone believes it *will* work." She glanced around. "If any of you can't believe, then don't feel you must stay. I know this probably sounds absolutely mad, but I have to try. Avendale was a very strong force. I believe his spirit would fight going into the hereafter."

"I'm sure you're right," Catherine said.

"Your Grace?"

She turned to look at Mrs. Ponsby. Her hair was black except for a white streak of strands that began at her widow's peak and trailed back, to be finally tucked into her bun. She wore a modest black dress that buttoned to her throat with tight sleeves that buttoned at her wrists. She couldn't be hiding anything there. She'd brought no instruments of her trade—no box into which she'd disappear while communing with the dead, no assistant, no magical ball or Ouija board. Winnie liked that she wasn't about the trappings. "Yes, Mrs. Ponsby?"

"We're almost ready. We just need something personal of your husband's."

"Oh. His rings would be perfect, but a servant must have put them away. I'll see if I can locate them."

"I have them," William said, pulling them from his pocket. "I knew they were upsetting you so I decided to tuck them away." He handed them over to the medium.

"These will do nicely. Please come join me at the table."

They did as requested. Winnie sat on her left, with William beside her, while Catherine sat on the medium's right. Mrs. Ponsby placed the rings on the table with the ducal crest turned toward her. Mrs. Ponsby signaled to a servant who went about the room, dimming the gaslights and extinguishing the flames in lamps until all the light came from a solitary candle on the table. Then all the servants quietly took their leave.

"We must all clasp each other's hands to form a circle of serenity into which the spirit will fill free to enter," she said quietly. "No matter what happens, you must not break the connection."

Hands were joined and Winnie felt her pulse thrumming.

"Avendale," Mrs. Ponsby sang in a voice that rose and fell like a wind blowing through the leaves. "Avendale, we know you're an unhappy spirit, unwilling to move to the beyond, that you are trying to make your presence known. We're here for you. Through me, you may speak with those in this room." Squeezing Winnie's hand, she closed her eyes and dropped her head back. "I am your vessel. Come to me."

Winnie waited. She knew what was supposed to happen next. According to her aunt, there would be a knocking, a cold draft along her neck, the hairs on her nape would prickle.

"Avendale," Mrs. Ponsby sang again. "Don't be shy. We're waiting for you. You need not be agitated with your present circumstance. We shall help you come to peace with it."

They waited. Mrs. Ponsby sang some more. They waited. More singing, a bit of moaning, a sigh. Mrs. Ponsby finally opened her eyes and looked at Winnie. "I'm sorry, Your Grace, but I don't sense that his spirit is about."

Winnie couldn't have been more disappointed if Mrs. Ponsby told her she would soon find herself residing in the spirit world alongside her husband. "Can't you try again? It would be just like him to be obstinate."

Mrs. Ponsby appeared somber. "There's a void where he should be. I can't explain it, but I can't contact him. He's just not there."

"But how can that be?" Winnie asked.

Mrs. Ponsby folded her hands on the table and looked at Winnie through kind eyes. "The only possible explanation is that he isn't dead."

G raves watched as all the blood drained from Winnie's face. Although only a candle provided light, within the dancing shadows she was starkly white. He didn't know what kind of game the medium was playing. She seemed so earnest, so honest. It made no sense.

"That's utterly ridiculous," he barked.

"Quite so," Claybourne said sternly. "He died in a fire at my ancestral estate. There can no doubt."

"But I must doubt," Mrs. Ponsby stated serenely, "as I don't sense his spirit in the afterworld."

It occurred to Graves that perhaps Avendale had gotten to the woman, paid her for this little performance in order to unsettle Winnie more. She was a fraud. All conjurers of the spirit world were frauds. He had to ensure that Winnie didn't begin to doubt her husband's death. He had to discredit the woman in some way.

"You're saying that you always manage to contact the spirits?" Catherine asked, lacing her voice with a healthy dose of skepticism.

"Indeed I do. This failure is a first for me and I am as baffled as the duchess. I can think of no other explanation."

"Perhaps the spirits are simply laying low tonight," Graves suggested.

"I think that unlikely. However, I am more than willing to try to contact someone else in an attempt to prove I'm not a fraud as I can sense from your demeanor that you believe I am up to no good. I assure you that I seek more to put the living to rest than the dead. As a physician, Dr. Graves, I'm sure you've seen more than your share of death. Is there someone you have lost with whom you would like to speak?"

For a heartbeat, a solitary heartbeat, he believed that she could do as she claimed. He thought of his father, of how he wanted to know what had happened to him, why he had left Graves all those nights ago. But for all he knew, the man was still alive. No, he needed someone who was very dead. "My mother."

"Have you an object that belongs to her?"

Reaching beneath his collar, he took hold of a pewter chain, slowly pulled it over his head. He placed it and the cross with the raised vines woven over it in Mrs. Ponsby's outstretched hand.

"Your mother was a religious woman," she mused.

"Very. She spent most of her time striving to beat the devil out of me."

"Those with strong religious convictions are the easiest to reach. Her name?"

He'd not thought it in years. "Flora Littleton."

He wasn't certain what his face showed, but he felt Winnie squeeze his hand where it sat fisted on the table. For a moment he'd forgotten that anyone else was there. It was Mrs. Ponsby's damn eyes. One brown, one blue. They drew a person in and held him enthralled.

"All right then," she said in a melodic voice. "We shall all join hands again and strive to make contact with Flora."

"Are you sure you want to do this?" Claybourne asked.

Graves held Mrs. Ponsby's gaze. "Yes, but I will not be convinced she's truly made contact unless my mother tells her something that only I know. Otherwise, it's cheap parlor tricks and she'll return to the duchess every ha'penny she took from her for tonight's entertainment."

"We have a bargain," she replied, and he was left with the sense that he'd made it with the devil's own mistress.

After they took hands, the medium dropped her head back, closed her eyes, and began to chant, "Flora Littleton come to us. Your son wishes to have words. He wants to re-connect with you. He wants you here."

Her voice drifted into a musical hum. He could almost sense a charge in the air; the hairs on his arms rose. Mrs. Ponsby went silent, then fell forward onto the table like a child's cloth doll. He started to reach for her, but Winnie clutched his hand.

"Mustn't break the circle," she whispered.

Inhaling a deep breath, Mrs. Ponsby rolled her back until she sitting straight up. Her pupils were completely dilated. Something was wrong. He broke free of Winnie's grasp, scraped back his chair—

"Your mother doesn't believe you want to speak with her," Mrs. Ponsby said calmly, "but she wants you to know that she forgives you for killing her."

CHAPTER SEVEN

Within the library, Graves poured himself a whiskey, tossed back his head, and downed it all. The medium's performance made no sense to him. Could it be that she was actually capable of communing with the dead? If she were a charlatan, why hadn't she pretended to contact Avendale? Her reputation, the amount of payment she could demand, was dependent upon her success at reaching the spirits.

And how the bloody hell had she known that he'd been responsible for his mother's death?

Downing an additional glass of whiskey, he felt another fissure of anger rip through him. After Mrs. Ponsby revealed his mother's supposed message, he'd come up out of the chair with a vengeance, knocking it over in the process. He wasn't exactly certain what he'd planned to do or say. He knew only that he'd needed to throw something, to walk from the room, to escape the demons of his past.

But Winnie had flinched and cowed, damn her.

"I wouldn't have struck you," he said now, hating the way

his voice seethed with emotions. He felt as though he were four years old, being battered by his mother again.

"I know," Winnie said softly. "My reaction was formed by habit. I know it upset you. I'm sorry for that."

"No matter how angry I get, I do not lash out with my fists." He'd fought back once and his mother had died as a result. He avoided confrontation at all cost.

"Yes, I know that as well," she said softly.

Following his reaction, the medium had excused herself, saying she was late for another appointment. Satisfaction shimmered off her, as she walked from the room without uttering any other word. Catherine and Claybourne had also taken their leave shortly thereafter. And Graves had headed straightaway for the liquor. He took another long gulp. He hadn't been able to protect himself when he was a child, but he damned sure wanted to protect Winnie.

"Perhaps we should adjourn to another room," she suggested.

"The whiskey's here and I'm in need of whiskey. Would you care for a brandy?"

She glanced around. "I don't like this room. It feels like he's here, as though he's watching us."

"He's not. Spirits do not come back to haunt us." Or at least that's what he had believed before tonight. Grabbing his glass, he strode over to the fireplace, pressed his forearm against the mantel, and stared into the fire. All these years, he'd managed to hold thoughts of his past at bay. He'd worked obsessively to save lives so he didn't have to focus on the one he'd taken.

Out of the corner of his eye, he watched as Winnie studied the table where the candle continued to burn, the shadows dancing around the rings and the pewter necklace. Even though the gaslights were now on, the candle seemed to provide more light. She brought her shoulders back, shoring up her courage he had no doubt. She marched over to the table, snatched up the rings, and walked to the desk. Opening the cigar box on the corner, she dropped the rings inside.

"Out of sight, out of mind?" he asked.

"Something like that."

She wandered back over to the table and picked up the necklace. As she approached him, he was grateful to see no hesitancy in her step, no wariness in her eyes. Stopping before him, she gave him a soft smile as she lifted the chain to place it around his neck. Bending his head, he relished the feel of her fingers skimming over his hair as she carried the chain down to rest against his neck. She patted the pewter that now hovered over his chest. "I think it's very sweet that you wear your mother's cross."

"Sweetness has nothing to do with it. It's so I never forget how quickly and easily death can come." His father had given it to him. "So you'll remember," he'd said, and he was fairly certain what it was his father wanted him to remember. Because of him his mother was dead.

Using only the tip of her finger, she touched the pewter again, and he imagined the tips of her fingers skipping over his chest, lingering here and there. "As soon as Mrs. Ponsby implied that you killed your mother, I knew the foolishness of thinking that anyone could truly contact the dead." She lifted her gaze to his. "I know you had nothing at all to do with your mother's death."

Only he had everything to do with it, but he couldn't tell her that. He didn't want to see the same fear in her eyes that he had seen in his father's.

"How did she know her words would strike a cord with you?" she asked.

She was so damned trusting, being this near to him, touching him, looking into his eyes. He wanted all of that: her trust, her touch, her deep brown eyes filled with adoration. For him, a sinner who had spent a good deal of his life striving to undo his sins. Wicked, his mother had called him, wicked boy, and he'd never understood exactly what he'd done that was so revolting. It had to be something inside of him, something only she could see.

"Because Mrs. Ponsby is very skilled at reading people. I have lost count of the number of times I have heard a parent say of their child, 'He will be the death of me.' I told her that my mother beat me. My mistake. I gave her something that she could work with. She would know that even if I had nothing at all to do with my mother's death, I would harbor some guilt over it because I would have wished her dead a thousand times."

"How do you know that she manipulates things in that way?"

"Because I grew up under the care of a kidsman who was very good at fleecing people. He would knock on someone's door, and within a matter of minutes he would know what sort of tale to weave in order to separate a man from his coins. Reading people is a skill that one can develop."

"Are you skilled at reading people?"

"It comes in handy when I have to deliver unpleasant news, if I can gauge how best to deliver it."

"Can you read me?" she asked.

He tried not to, didn't want to know exactly what she was thinking, how she felt. "I know you're afraid."

"Not of you. I've never been afraid of you. I know you're a good man."

Only he wasn't. His past was a labyrinth of wrongdoing. His redemption rested with her, if he could only protect her from her husband, protect her from himself.

But she was making it so difficult when she stepped in closer, until her body was flush with his. She may have well have laid a hot brand to his flesh. He was acutely aware of every luscious dip and curve that comprised her.

He was familiar with the human body, had examined hundreds of them, had examined her, but he had never wanted to explore one with the patience and depths that he wanted to explore hers. He wanted to know the smallest of details, slide his tongue along the tiniest of crevices. He wanted to become lost in her until he forgot his past, until hers could no longer create a chasm between them. He wanted what he could not have, what he should not take.

But at that moment he needed the surcease she could offer, the balm of her innocence, the solace of her trust.

Cupping her face, he planted his mouth over hers. Triumph rushed through him as she sagged against him, an invitation he could no longer ignore. He would have regrets in the morning. He had little doubt she would as well, but tonight they were both raw and wounded, reeling from disappointment, despair. The unexpected turn of events.

He lifted her into his arms. "Not in here," he said, "not in here where the ghosts from both our pasts linger."

With resolve in his stride, William carried Winnie through the house with purpose. She should have objected. Any decent woman would, but she wanted too badly what he was offering, and she wanted to provide comfort in return. She had thought tonight she would be dealing with her past, and it seemed he was dealing with his.

She was glad she'd had a chance to see him in anger—in fury, more like. She knew for certain that he would never take his fists to her, would never hurt her. She could trust him with her body—and in doing so, with her heart and soul. He would guard them, he would keep them safe.

It was late, and all the servants were abed. She was grateful for that, although she wasn't certain it would have mattered. As she kissed the underside of his jaw, she realized how very desperately she wanted to be with him.

He opened the door to her bedchamber, walked through, then slammed it shut with his foot. Setting her down on the bed, he stretched out beside her, rising up on one elbow. As one of his fingers journeyed along her throat and stopped at the first button, she held her breath.

His eyes darkened, his breathing grew shallow. "It will be like seeing you for the first time."

He'd seen her injuries, but not the scars that had formed. Could she share them with him? Could she share them with anyone? They shamed her and yet—

"I don't find scars hideous," he said as though reading her thoughts. Leaning in he kissed her brow. "The reason behind them perhaps, but they are a badge of survival." He pressed his lips to the small one at her cheek. "But you have scars across your soul, and I don't know how to heal those." He touched his tongue to a small place beneath her chin.

Was there a scar there as well? It seemed he knew her better than she knew herself, but then he had treated them while she had avoided looking for any reminders of that night.

"Do you have scars?" she asked.

"A few, from when I was a boy, so they are faint now. You probably wouldn't even notice them, but I still see them, feel them, know they are there. We look at ourselves more harshly than others do. We think people note the imperfections because they are glaring to us, when in fact they are nothing at all to others."

With little more than a quick flick of his wrist, he freed the first button.

Stop him, a tiny voice cried, but a louder one told her she would be a fool not to welcome his advances. She remembered how gently he had tended her hurts, how tenderly he had changed bandages and applied salve.

Now he cupped her face, leaned in, and captured her mouth in a deep searing kiss that sent all her doubts, her inhibitions to perdition. Within her he stirred a matching hunger that she couldn't deny. She wanted his mouth, his hands, his body, every aspect of him touching her, becoming part of her. She'd never felt this way before, had never dared want anything this desperately.

She was vaguely aware of the other buttons being released. Pulling back slightly, he slowly peeled away her bodice, his eyes fastened on the skin he was revealing. She saw appreciation wash over his features, and she felt treasured, beautiful, accepted.

Within a few heartbeats, he had her stripped of her clothes. She watched in wonder as he quickly divested himself of his clothing. She saw no scars, but then the whole of him was distractingly marvelous. Hard muscles, flat stomach, narrow hips.

Rejoining her, he took his mouth on a sojourn over her body, pressing a healing kiss to each scar, the ones along her ribs, her collarbone, her thigh. He licked, kissed, murmured sweet words. Then he kissed the whole of her. Every inch, every nook and cranny, every hidden cove.

When he returned his mouth to hers, she was heated with need, burning with desire. She plowed her hands into his hair, relishing the feel of the soft curls claiming her fingers, wrapping around them. She turned her body into his, skimming the sole of her foot along his calf. She moved in rhythm with him, rolling one way and another, striving to touch all of him as he touched all of her. There was no complacency from either of them.

For the first time in her life she felt as though she were an equal partner in the lovemaking. Nothing she did disappointed him. Nothing she did was incorrect. She explored to her heart's content. Exultation swept through her when he groaned deeply, and she felt the vibrations of his chest. She had caused that reaction, and she felt triumphant. He cradled one breast. His eyes fluttered closed, long dark lashes resting on his cheeks. He lowered his head and circled his tongue around her nipple, taunting and teasing.

The first gentle tug almost had her coming off the bed. No pain, just sweet sensations surging through her. He gave his attentions to her other breast, to the valley between, to her stomach, and lower. Everywhere he touched cried out for release, she cried out for release.

Then he rose above her, gazed down on her. She locked her eyes onto his as he eased himself inside her, withdrawing slightly, pushing with more determination, over and over until he was nestled deeply inside her.

He rocked against her. She met each thrust, the pleasure increasing, until she was writhing beneath him and screaming out for release. It came in a glorious rush that had her bucking against him, as he groaned hoarsely and drove into her one last time.

Exhausted and replete, she lay beneath him, skimming lethargic fingers over his damp back, aware of the trembling in his arms as he kept his weight off her, a consideration that touched her deeply. He pressed his lips to her temple before rolling off her. He drew her up against his side, stroking her arm as though he was as loath to lose contact with her as she was to lose it with him. As his breathing slowed, he kissed the top of her head. "I'm not leaving tonight, so sleep as deeply as you want."

Inhaling sandalwood and the musk of their lovemaking, she closed her eyes.

Winnie decided that she rather enjoyed being made love to in the morning. It was a glorious thing to wake up to. Then they'd enjoyed breakfast in bed before satisfying each other once again. She couldn't recall if she'd ever known such happiness.

She also discovered that she liked being dressed by a man,

even if her hair was nothing more than a simple braid. Sitting at her dressing table, she watched as William put on his shoes. She'd never observed a man getting completely dressed before. She rather liked all these new experiences.

"I suppose you have to take your leave now," she said.

Standing, he walked over to her and brought her to her feet. "I'm taking a day of leisure, to do nothing beyond being with you."

"What of your patients?"

"No one is knocking on death's door. My housekeeper knows where I am. If a hospital needs me, they'll send word 'round to her and she'll send word to me." He cradled her cheek. "I want to be with you."

"I promised Whit I'd take him to Madame Tussaud's."

"I'll accompany you."

She couldn't deny the pleasure that his offer brought her, although a secret part of her had to admit that she'd rather stay abed with him. She'd never in her life felt so treasured, so appreciated, so cared for. This was how it was supposed to be between a man and a woman. If Avendale hadn't died, she'd have never known.

But she also recognized that there was more to William's treatment of her. It made her stronger, it made her believe that she should be treated better. A small part, a very small part of her wished she could confront Avendale and show him that she wasn't the cowering girl he'd married.

"Let's share the news with Whit."

But before she could leave the room, William took her into his arms again and kissed her as though he hadn't spent a good portion of the night doing just that. She wound her arms around his neck, knowing she would never tire of this. Although she had secured no promises from him, she understood now that she didn't require marriage to be happy. It was enough just to be with him.

When he broke away and opened the door for her, she knew a secretive little smile played over her lips and hoped that Whit couldn't interpret its meaning.

As they walked down the hallway, William said, "I'd have not expected you to be a fan of Madame Tussaud's."

"I must admit that I think I might have gone mad making wax creations of the deceased, but I find it fascinating to see people as they were. Although I do avoid the torture chamber." She knew enough about the grisly room to know she had no desire to see instruments of torture or to see them demonstrated on wax figurines, even if they could feel no pain.

"It's my understanding," William said, "that ladies aren't allowed in the room because of their delicate sensibilities."

"Have you ever been in there?"

"No, I've seen enough suffering in life not to want to see it in wax."

"How do you bear it, all the suffering you've seen?"

"By focusing on happier things, like moments spent with you."

He said such lovely things to her. She was half tempted to forego the trip with Whit and spend the entire day in her bedchamber with William, but she wanted him to have some time with her son. She knew they'd gotten along famously while she and Whit had stayed at William's residence during her recovery, but she thought it a good idea to reacquaint them as she suspected she would be spending a good deal more time with William.

She walked into the nursery, although it seemed odd to refer to it as such when Whit was all of seven years old now. He would soon be exchanging the nursery for the classroom, but for a bit longer he was hers.

Whit was sitting at a small table, frantically scratching a pencil over his art pad. Several sheets of paper were scattered around the table. His governess was sitting in a nearby chair reading. She quickly stood, but Whit carried on.

Winnie knelt beside him. "Good morning, darling."

"There were so many animals. I'm trying to draw them, before I forget what they looked like."

"You're doing a marvelous job. Perhaps you'd like to share them with Dr. Graves. He's visiting this morning. You remember him, don't you?"

Whit looked up then, his dark hair falling across his brow, his dark eyes—his father's eyes—focusing on William. "You took care of Mummy when she was hurt."

She did wish that he didn't remember that particular aspect of their time with William. Whit had been only four. She hoped he'd have forgotten the worst of if by now.

"You carried me on your shoulders in the park," Whit continued.

William crouched beside her. "Yes, I did. I'd like to take you and your mum to the park again sometime, but I understand you already have a special trip planned for today."

"Have to finish these first."

"Did you like walking through the zoological gardens?" William asked.

Whit nodded, his hair flapping against his brow. He pointed to one of the papers. "That's the lion. He roared."

"It's a very good drawing," William said, picking it up and holding it so Winnie could see it clearly. The lion's mane was almost larger than the lion himself. Off to the side was a tree. Near it was something that appeared to be an obelisk: tall and dark, no features. With a quick glance over the other sketches, she saw that it appeared in several of them. She didn't know why she found it odd, but she did. In one of the drawings, it seemed to have arms.

"What is this, darling?" she asked.

Whit's tiny brow furrowed as he studied where her finger rested, before darting his gaze up to her. "It's the shadow man."

Everything within her stilled while he returned to his endeavors as though he hadn't said anything monumental. "What shadow man?" She hated the slight tremor in her voice. She was very much aware that William hadn't moved, but he seemed alert, barely breathing.

Whit lifted a slender shoulder. "I've seen him about. Sometimes in the park. The garden."

"Our garden?" Winnie asked.

Whit nodded.

She looked over at the governess. "Have you seen him?"

"No, Your Grace. The young duke has mentioned him of course, but he has such an active imagination that I assumed the shadow man was an imaginary friend."

Yes, that was probably it, Winnie thought. Just a figment—

"He was in my room last night," Whit said distractedly, his attention back on his drawing. "I woke up and he was in the shadows. I couldn't see him very well, but he said he was watching out for me and not to be afraid. This is the elephant."

He held the paper out to her, and she took it with trembling fingers. Last night, dear God, last night when she was crying out in pleasure, he was in her residence, in her son's room. "He's a very interesting creature with that long snout. So your shadow man, did he say anything else?"

He shook his head. "But he was wearing my rings."

"Your rings?"

He nodded. "The ones you said I can wear when I'm a man."

She had shown the ducal rings to Whit several times because he enjoyed looking at them.

"I didn't tell him they were mine," Whit said quietly. "'Cuz he was so big."

Leaning over, she pressed a kiss to his temple. "He won't hurt you, darling. Mummy isn't feeling well, though, so we're not going on our outing today. You just keep drawing."

Her legs were trembling so badly they could barely support her as she left the room. What she was considering was an impossibility, and yet it was the only thing that made any sense.

"Winnie, are you all right?" William asked.

"Hardly." With William on her heels, she rushed down the stairs and hurried into the library, went to the cigar box where she had placed the rings after the séance, and lifted the lid. They were gone. After slamming the lid closed, she began striding toward the door. "I need to speak with Catherine. My husband either managed to manifest himself into a ghost or he was never dead to begin with."

Chapter Eight

"Tell me precisely what happened at Heatherwood," Winnie demanded.

William knew that he could have saved her the journey to Claybourne's, but it wasn't his lie to reveal. They were in the Claybourne library, a room large enough that with the door closed, it was unlikely that any of their conversation would drift out into the hallways to be overheard by servants. They were presently all standing, Claybourne in front of his desk, his hips leaning against it, Catherine near her husband. Winnie stood before them, her hands balled into fists at her side. At least they'd stopped trembling on the journey here. He wanted to be beside her, holding her near, but she seemed determined to face this on her own, so he merely waited, his arms crossed over his chest. It was her battle.

"Why don't we all take a seat?" Catherine asked. "I'll ring for tea."

"I don't want tea," Winnie said. "I want to know about the fire at Heatherwood. Did you actually see Avendale die in it?"

Catherine glanced over at Claybourne before returning

her attention to Winnie. "Winnie, you must understand that I was terrified for you."

"What did you do?" she asked, her voice laced with trepidation.

"Do sit," Catherine urged.

"I don't think I shall. I have the impression that what you are about to tell me is best taken standing."

Good for you, William thought, admiring her backbone. Her husband had nearly broken it. He hoped she'd hang onto it when she knew the true tale.

Catherine cleared her throat. "The night he beat you to within an inch of your life, before we left your residence, we hinted to the servants that we were going to take you to Heatherwood. Instead, of course, we took you to Bill. Then Claybourne and I carried on alone to Heatherwood."

"Avendale arrived a couple of nights later demanding that we give you to him. When he learned you weren't there, he went into a rage, attacked Claybourne. In the scuffle a burning lamp shattered on the floor, the kerosene and flames igniting the carpet and draperies. Claybourne got the upper hand and knocked Avendale unconscious. But by the time he did, the fire was raging. While I take no pride in it, I was grateful that he didn't have the means to escape the fire."

"So he did die, you left him to die."

Catherine hesitated. "Winnie—"

"For God's sake tell her the truth," William snapped, "because if you don't I will."

Her brow deeply furrowed, Winnie jerked her gaze over to him, and not averting his was the hardest thing he'd ever done.

"Claybourne carried him out," Catherine said on a rush, snagging Winnie's attention once more.

"So he didn't die?"

Sadly Catherine shook her head.

Winnie stumbled back a couple of steps. "But I saw the body."

"You saw *a* body, dressed in Avendale's clothes, wearing his rings. We arranged for Avendale to be transported to New Zealand as a criminal, under another name. We can only deduce that he either managed to escape or convinced someone to set him free."

"You can only deduce? So you believe he's here, wreaking havoc with my sanity, and you didn't think I needed to know?"

Catherine nodded reluctantly. "We believed we could handle it without you being the wiser for it. You thought you were a widow—"

Winnie staggered back as though she'd taken a blow. Horrified, she looked at William and he knew she was thinking of last night, of her marriage vows, of how she'd unwittingly broken them. "I'm not a widow. My son is not the duke."

"No one need know that," Catherine said. "We will find him. We will set matters to right."

"I think you all have done quite enough." She slowly turned to face William squarely. "You robbed graves in your youth, so I assume you provided the body. Where did you get it?"

"Potter's Field."

"A pauper is buried in my husband's family's crypt?"

While it brought him no pride, he nodded.

"All along you knew he was alive. Last night—" Tears welled in her eyes. "You knew I wasn't a widow. You knew I wasn't . . . free."

He had no response whatsoever to that accusation. He had known, damn him, and he'd put his needs to have her above all else.

She advanced on him. "I thought I was going mad. Things disappearing, reappearing. Sounds in the night. His scent wafting through the house, which I now realize must have been wafting in his wake. He was in my son's room. He was in *my* room. You knew all this and yet you let me doubt my sanity."

"You can't blame him," Catherine said. "When we decided to do this, we took a vow of secrecy."

Winnie's gaze never left his. "A vow more important than me." Then she laughed, a sound that carried no joy. "Your attentions of late, were they all part of this elaborate scheme to hide what you'd done, to ensure I didn't learn the truth?"

Easier to lie than to tell her the truth because at this point she wouldn't believe him anyway. "I wanted to be certain I was there to protect you should he show himself."

"You left me to suffer. You didn't trust me not to betray you."

"Winnie, you wept when I told you he was dead," Catherine said.

"Of course I wept. With profound relief because no one would ever hurt me again." She turned back to William. "Although I was mistaken there. How was I to know the pain of broken bones pales in comparison to that of a broken heart?"

"Winnie, it was never my intention to hurt you."

She gave a caustic laugh. "Do you know that Avendale said those precise words after every time he hit me?"

Nothing else she could have said would have cut him as deeply.

Glancing quickly at the others, she said, "Please, I beg you all, don't help me any further. I shall see to this matter myself."

With her chin held high, she marched from the room, marched out of his life. He let her go because he knew he had killed whatever love she might have held for him.

He was vaguely aware of Catherine touching his arm. "What she said, it wasn't fair."

"It was completely fair."

Avendale was alive!

Winnie let that thought hover around her as she sat in his hideous overbearing library. He was alive. She wasn't free. She wasn't free to love William. She wasn't free to even kiss him!

Why hadn't Avendale walked into the residence and announced his return?

Because he wanted to toy with her, the bastard. He no doubt blamed her for what he had suffered. As much as she wished Catherine hadn't taken such drastic measures to keep Winnie safe, she also had to admit that she was touched by her friend's devotion. Angry to be sure, disappointed that they had thought they couldn't trust her, but also touched.

Three years ago, she'd been too shy to stand up for herself, had lacked confidence in her abilities. Had even thought on occasion that perhaps she deserved the rough treatment. But now she understood that Avendale had no right to pommel his fists into her, no right to treat her badly. That he thought he could return and begin to torment her anew was not to be tolerated.

She considered packing her things and taking Whit someplace where they would both be safe, but she didn't like the way it made her feel to avoid the confrontation that she was certain would be happening very soon. So she had his governess take him to a cousin's for a few days. She gave the servants the night off. With the doors to the library open onto the terrace, she watched as evening fell, all the while feeling as though she were being watched.

Sooner or later he would face her, she was certain of it. He could have his place in Society back. But he could not have his place back in her life. Although it would create enormous scandal, she would divorce him. Or more precisely, have him divorce her for adultery. She would admit to sleeping with William Graves. Her butler could testify that he possessed a key so he could come and go as he pleased. She suspected William would confess to the wrongdoing as well. After all, he owed her.

But regardless, she was not going to stay in this marriage.

During Avendale's time away, she had come into her own. She managed the household here in London and at the estates and she managed them well. She had put together the means to raise money for a hospital. She had spoken with architects and builders and a physician in order to discover all that was needed. They had talked with her, offered advice, took her suggestions. She no longer felt small or insignificant. She was confident she could manage her own affairs. She'd been doing quite nicely for three years.

Thanks to William Graves, who had shown her how it should be between a man and a woman. Even before his interest of late, when she had been recovering, and had first suggested the notion for a hospital, he had embraced it and never questioned her ability to carry it off. He treated her with respect and valued her.

She could not go back to flinching every time her husband spoke, to cowering when he came near, to expecting to receive a blow.

While it occurred to her that things might go better if she had all her friends surrounding her, she needed to take care of this matter on her own. They had already put their lives and reputations at risk. Her anger at them was dissipating, leaving her overwhelmed with the realization that they would risk so much for her.

When it was her battle to fight.

Graves knew he shouldn't be standing behind the hedgerows that lined Winnie's back gardens, that she despised him and didn't want him near, but he couldn't force himself to stay away, not when there was a chance that she might be hurt, that her husband might be lurking in the shadows.

Whatever had made any of them think that their plan would be a permanent solution to Winnie's problem, and why had they all agreed to it without consulting her? Why had he taken a role in it?

Because examining her bloody, battered, and smashed

body, he had believed, truly believed, that no one should be mistreated as she had been. She had been so small, delicate, and fragile that it had never occurred to him that she would be capable of taking care of herself. Shame on him for not seeing three years ago that all she needed was to develop the confidence to stand up for herself. She had been so determined this morning to brush them off, to make it on her own.

But making it on her own, taking care of the matter, meant facing her husband, and he couldn't allow her to face him alone. No matter how strong she thought she was, she was not strong enough for that.

He'd seen the servants leaving earlier, assumed her son had been taken elsewhere. No light escaped from any of the windows except the ones that looked out from the library. She was preparing to meet the beast in his own lair. He wondered if Avendale would respond to the invitation. Surely he had to know by now that she was aware he had returned.

Graves heard something rustling off to his left. Hefting the cudgel he'd borrowed from Jim, he cautiously stepped forward and peered—

Pain shot through the back of his skull.

Then nothing.

"Hello, duchess."

Winnie didn't remember falling asleep in the chair by the fire, but the smooth ominous voice sent a tremor through her. Fighting down the fear, she opened her eyes.

A great hulk of a man was crouched before her. Avendale. Only it wasn't. This man bore a horrid scar from cheek to chin. He was unshaven, his hair an unruly mess. His clothing was not tailored to fit him but looked like something he might have taken from a beggar. He wore a coarse black coat. His arms were beefier, his hands rougher.

"Avendale," she replied, grateful her voice was steady. "Fancy seeing you here."

"I think you were expecting me, but I still managed to take your lover by surprise."

"My lover? I don't know what you're talking about."

He shifted slightly and she saw William lying on the carpet, his hands bound behind him, eyes closed, blood pooling at the back of his head. "My God, what did you do?"

She started to get up, to see how badly he was injured, but Avendale shoved her back into the chair with one meaty hand, and rose to tower over her like Lucifer ascending from hell. "Were you bedding him before I was sent away?"

"I was never unfaithful."

"What do you call last night? I stood outside your bedchamber listening to your cries. I almost barged in to kill him then and there, to kill you both. I would have been within my rights."

"I thought you were dead. I didn't know what happened to you, not until today."

"You expect me to believe that?"

"I really don't care if you do or not. Why have you been lurking about in such an unmanly fashion?" His jaw tightened and she could see the red flush of embarrassment staining his skin. If there was anything that irked him more than having his manhood questioned, she didn't know what it was. Well, maybe being sent to the far side of the world aboard a prison ship was considerably more irritating. "Why not announce your return, why play these silly games?"

"So no one would question my sending my devoted wife to an insane asylum. My wife who loses things and finds them, who believes in spirits." He grabbed the arms of the chair and lowered himself until he was hovering an inch from her nose. "I enjoyed watching you panic, although I must confess that you didn't break as quickly as I thought you would."

"You watched the séance last night, didn't you? And afterward. That's how you knew where to find your rings."

He grinned. "I almost answered the lady's summons, but better not to let others know I was about—not just yet anyway."

"Why do this?"

"To punish you and Catherine. Maybe she'll even go mad with guilt, thinking of you spending the rest of your life among the truly insane."

"If you want to be rid of me, simply divorce me."

"Where's the fun in that?"

"Why not kill me then as you did your other wives?"

A corner of his mouth hitched up sinisterly. "You can't prove I killed them."

"But you did, didn't you? No one is going to believe a madwoman, so why not tell me? Maybe knowing I was married to a murderer will be enough to send me over the edge."

He released something between a grunt and a laugh. "I'd almost think you'd acquired some spunk while I was gone. That would be a shame as it would mean your permanent demise."

It bothered her that he would think she would break so

easily. But if she'd been tougher before, perhaps he would have killed her. "You did kill them then."

"Of course I did. They were barren. I needed an heir. Divorce is costly, time consuming, and scandalous. Now I have an heir, I'm in no need of a wife, especially one who can't be trusted. After what I've been through, you deserve to suffer a bit. Do you know what it's like on those prison hulks? I got infested with fleas and lice. Fleas and lice for God's sake. And a rat actually bit me before I snapped its scrawny little neck."

His eyes were wide, glittering, and she wondered if perhaps his ordeal had made him mad. Perhaps he was the one who belonged in an asylum.

"They made me work until my hands bled and my back ached. They laughed when I told them I was a duke. Took a lash to me. It was almost two years before I found a way to escape. And all the while I plotted my revenge. Then last night I heard you with *him*, and I realized he would have to be punished as well."

"You might want to rethink that. He serves the queen."

"It'll just look like he ran into a rough lot who beat him to death and left him in the mews."

She fought back her fear. She would not allow him to hurt William. "No."

"You can't stop me. You've always been a frightened little bird whose wings were clipped. When I'm done with him, I plan to spend the night getting reacquainted with my wife before sending her off to Bedlam."

Her stomach roiled as she thought of him touching her, of him wiping away the touch of a man she loved. She did love William, in spite of what he had hidden from her, she loved him. Wasn't he the one who had insisted Catherine tell her the truth? He'd known she was strong enough to handle it. He knew everything about her, inside and out, and he accepted her as she was.

"Go to hell," she said and shoved on his chest. The great hulk that was her husband barely moved. He just laughed, laughed as he had when he'd hit her before, when she cried out. She'd learned not to cry out.

A growl echoed around them. Winnie barely had time to register the sight of William charging before he knocked Avendale aside. Both men tumbled to the floor. Still bound, William struggled to stand. Avendale had nothing to hamper his progress. Jumping to his feet, he grabbed William by the shirt front, lifted him slightly, and pounded his fist into his face.

She heard the crack of bone shattering, a sound that had once echoed between her ears as her own bones took the weight of his fists. Jumping from the chair, she grabbed the fireplace poker and smashed it across his back. He spun around. She put all her strength, her weight, her need to stop him in the next swing, catching him across the head, sending him off balance. He landed on his back at the stone edge of the fireplace, his head at an awkward angle, leaning against his gargoyle.

Breathing heavily, she stood, feet spread, poker at the ready to strike him again. But he didn't move. He just lay there staring at her as though he were surprised that she'd fought back this time.

"Untie me."

She jerked her gaze over to William as he struggled to sit

up, blood gushing from his nose. "Oh, yes, of course." As she knelt beside him and fumbled with the knots, she kept darting glances over at Avendale. "How did he come to have you?"

"I was in the garden, keeping watch, but I was foolish enough to fall for his trick. Are you hurt?"

"No, not really. He seemed more intent on talking me to death."

William released a huff that might have been a laugh. When his arms were free, he cradled her face. "You were extraordinarily brave."

"I never stood up to him before, never fought back. I couldn't return to living like that. I wouldn't. But I think I hurt him rather badly."

"I'll have a look."

She watched as William moved over to Avendale. "Be careful," she warned.

"He won't hurt me." He pressed his ear to Avendale's chest, then gently lifted Avendale's head. She saw the blood seeping onto the stone.

"Looks as though he took quite a blow. I should get some linens to stanch the bleeding," she said.

William moved back over to her, folded his hands over her shoulders, and met her gaze. "Winnie, he's dead."

Winnie sat in a chair in a corner. After covering Avendale with a sheet, William had sent for Inspector Swindler. She watched as he first studied the door, then crouched down and lifted the sheet to examine Avendale.

"Obviously someone from the streets," he said.

"He's the Duke of Avendale," she corrected.

He looked at her, looked at William, looked at Avendale. "I see a man of the streets, a thief who has no doubt been breaking into your residence and stealing things. My report will indicate that the door has been tampered with by somewhat of an expert."

She was on the verge of protesting again, when it dawned on her why William had sent for Swindler. "Of course. You're part of the group that lived with the Earl of Claybourne's grandfather."

William took a step toward her. "Winnie, I know you despise me but no good will come from revealing the truth now. Swindler can make all this appear as though he broke in."

"Are you saying that to protect yourself?"

"No, to protect you from the scandal. Everything about your life with him will become fodder for gossip. Yes, there are those of us who will no doubt suffer because of what we did, but you also have to consider the impact the tale will have on your son."

She'd never spoken ill of Avendale to his son, had never wanted Whit to know the brute that his father was. He would suffer if the truth came out.

"But I killed him."

"Not really. You hit him. He fell. The blow to the head killed him, but you had no influence over that. It was an accident."

"Which is how my report will read," Swindler said. "With all due respect, Your Grace, no one will question my findings."

"You can live with this?"

"I can live with justice being served. In my profession, I see a lot of people who are hurt or killed and the culprits aren't always caught. So I take justice where I can. Your husband treated you poorly, almost killed you, probably would have killed Bill here tonight. He was a man who didn't feel remorse or regret. I'm not sorry to see him go. As I'm given to understand his two previous wives met with unfortunate accidents. Poetic justice, I say, that he should die from a blow to the head."

"Is it really? In convincing me to say nothing are you not also striving to protect yourself? I imagine you played some role in his incarceration. You would have had access to the prisons that none of the others had."

"We all knew the risks, Winnie," William said. "We were all prepared to live with the results if what we did was ever discovered. Do what you must."

She thought of how courageous they must have all been to risk so much when only Catherine truly knew her. What was she to them, other than someone the law wouldn't protect? So they had done what they could to protect her.

She took a deep breath, a long sigh. "He's wearing my husband's rings. I'm not certain when he stole them, but they belong to my son, are part of his inheritance."

Swindler nodded. "I'll add that to my report. I'll take the body to the coroner now if you have no objections."

"I want him buried in the family crypt," she informed them. "You don't have to remove the other fellow, but Avendale should rest with his ancestors."

"I'll see to that," William said.

She wasn't surprised by his offer. He'd been looking out for her longer than she'd known, and he also had the skills to manage the task by himself. "We should see to your injuries," she said.

"I'm fine."

"You don't look fine from here," Swindler said. "I'll finish up. You go let the lady tend you."

It appeared that William was going to object, so she said softly, "Please."

She couldn't have been more relieved when he acquiesced.

After taking him to her bedchamber, she sat him at her dressing table. She dipped a cloth into the washbasin, then kneeling before him began to gently wipe away the blood that he'd overlooked when he'd stopped the bleeding with his handkerchief. He grimaced, and she lightened her touch.

"I'm sorry if that hurt," she said.

"I'll live. I'm sorry that I didn't tell you what I suspected when you first told me about the strange happenings. I was hoping I was wrong."

She gave him a soft smile. "You'd rather I be mad?"

He shook his head. "No, I was hoping for another explanation."

"I'm relieved that it's over, that he's truly gone, and yet I'm melancholy."

"That's to be expected I think."

"If I hadn't hit him so hard—"

He cradled her face between his palms. "Winnie, make no mistake. He was going to kill me. Bound as I was, I doubt I could have stopped him. In spite of his plans to have you committed, I suspect he would have killed you as well. I heard a bit of your conversation with him. He practically confessed to killing his other wives. You acquired justice not only for you but for them."

"Will the guilt lessen in time, do you think?"

"I know it will, but it will never completely go away." He averted his gaze for a moment, a distant expression on his face, and she couldn't help but believe he was visiting the past. How often had she done the same? She watched as he swallowed. When he brought his gaze back to hers, it was raw, tormented. "Mrs. Ponsby had the right of it. I was responsible for my mother's death. She was beating me one day, at the top of our stairs, outside for all the world to see. I was huddled, trying to deflect the blows, and I struck out at her, tried to kick her. I'm unclear as to exactly how it happened, but our legs got tangled, she lost her balance, fell backward through the railing and landed in the street. Broke her neck."

She squeezed his hands. "Oh my God, my love, you can't blame yourself for what happened."

"I don't think I fully understood that until tonight when I saw you strike out at Avendale. You didn't mean to kill him, Winnie, just as I didn't mean to kill my mother. I've spent a good deal of my life striving to make amends for something that wasn't my fault. You are equally blameless in tonight's tragedy."

"Yes, but—" Somehow her situation felt different, but was it really?

"I think that's why my father left me that night," William continued. "When I gazed over the landing at my mother, I saw my father standing there, looking up at me. I think he might have feared that I was going to be like her, a brute. So he moved on."

How could his father have left him? How could he have believed for a single moment that William would turn out like his mother? It never crossed Winnie's mind that Whit would grow up to be anything except a good, honorable man.

"Although I never met him, I don't much like your father," she said. "That he would leave a child to fend for himself."

"But his actions resulted in my life taking a turn that led me here. I love you, Winnie. I have for three years now, but I held my affections at bay, because I didn't think you'd approve of what we'd done and that you would despise me for my role in it. But then I kissed you in the garden and all of that hardly seemed to matter anymore."

It didn't matter. They had tried to protect her because she hadn't been strong enough to protect herself. But that night and all the days that followed changed her. She would never again believe she deserved anything other than the best. She had no doubt that the man before her was the absolute best. She gave him a small smile.

"Well, I am truly a widow now."

He grinned at her. "So you are."

CHAPTER NINE

Six Months Later

Winnie thought a wedding was a fine way to begin the year, and so she was quite excited when the first week of January was finally upon them and she was studying her reflection in a mirror. She had sold the house in London—too many ghosts there—and moved into a modest home that William had purchased. That afternoon, he would officially take up residence here with her and Whit, although many a previous night he, scoundrel that he was, would sneak in and join her in bed or sit with her before a fire and they would talk into the wee hours of the morning. She loved every moment she spent in his company.

William had been quite attentive the past several months as she struggled to reconcile all that had happened and came to terms with it. Avendale's death often haunted her. Sometimes she awoke in a cold sweat, certain he'd arisen from the dead determined to reclaim her, but William was always there to comfort and assure her it was not so. He was gone, truly gone this time, and would never again hurt her.

She came to accept that Catherine had sought to protect

her as best she could. Winnie dealt with some guilt over placing her friend in a position where she was willing to sell her soul in order to prevent Winnie from suffering at her husband's hands. All she could remember during those long years was feeling helpless and not knowing where to turn.

But somehow, while Avendale had been away, she had changed, had taken charge of her own destiny. While she had not meant to kill him, she had fully intended to stand up to him, to show him that he could no longer control her with his fists. His returning had been her opportunity to redeem herself, to put him in his place, to demonstrate that she was now a woman to be reckoned with.

But all of those thoughts were for another day. Today, she was getting married.

"You look lovely," Catherine said, coming up behind her to settle the veil into place.

"I feel lovely, inside and out."

A rap sounded on the door. Catherine opened the door, and Winnie heard the Earl of Claybourne say, "It's beginning to snow. We'd best be off to the church."

Catherine turned to her. "Are you ready, Winnie?"

She took one last look at her reflection. She saw a woman who stood a bit taller, had no fears, was confident regarding the path she was on. A woman who was loved.

"More than ready."

As most of the aristocracy was still in the country, only a few people attended the ceremony. Graves didn't mind as they were the ones that mattered: Swindler and his wife,

Emma; Jack Dodger and Lady Olivia; Frannie and the Duke of Greystone. The Earl of Claybourne had stood with Graves while Catherine was beside Winnie.

After they were pronounced man and wife, they enjoyed breakfast with their friends, then returned to their residence where they had watched Whit romping in the snow. But now it was late, the house was quiet, and she was his.

Standing behind her at the vanity, he brushed her hair, loving the way the mahogany glistened. He thought he would never tire of it, or of gazing at her reflection in the mirror. It didn't hurt that she wasn't wearing any clothes. But then neither was he. It seemed pointless to go through the motions of putting on nightclothes when they would only be removed as soon as possible. He enjoyed gazing at her body, and was grateful that she didn't seem to mind giving his a once-over every now and then.

At the hundredth stroke, he swept the cascade of her hair over her shoulder, leaned down, and pressed a kiss to the nape of her neck. "I love you."

Her eyes sparkled and glowed. Turning on the low stool, she smiled up at him. "I love you, too."

Elegantly, she rose, skimming her body along his until her arms were wound around his neck and her lips were playing with his. Slipping his hands beneath her hips, he lifted her and she wrapped her legs around his waist. He suspected he would be rowing his boat for the next hundred years in order to keep his arms strong enough to carry her wherever he wanted her to be. Holding her near, he strode over to the bed and tumbled onto it, taking her down with him.

She shrieked, laughed. He loved to hear her laugh, and

of late it seemed she laughed more and more. She was free of cares, free of worries. She lightened his days, eased his burdens, brought joy to his nights. How had he ever thought he could go a lifetime without her to share moments with?

He had been consumed with healing, not realizing that a part of him needed healing as well. He didn't need to save the world to atone for the sins of his youth. He merely needed to save a portion of it. He'd only needed to save her.

But in the end, she had saved him.

With Swindler's report, no one became suspicious regarding the thief who had broken into the residence and subsequently died. No one suspected Winnie of any wrongdoing. As a matter of fact, she had been heralded as quite the heroine for not being cowed by an intruder. While she blushed at the praise and downplayed it, he could not deny that she had changed into a woman who knew she deserved far better than her husband was giving her. Three and half years ago, her husband had nearly killed her, but she had arisen from the ashes of that beating to become a stronger, more confident woman, one who understood her own worth. He couldn't be more grateful that she didn't need him to rescue her, although that didn't mean that he wouldn't always be near to watch over her.

He took his hands and mouth over the familiar terrain of her body, relishing every inch. There was comfort in the familiar, in knowing that any further changes would happen because of nature and the passing years. No one would ever hurt her again. No one would ever hurt him. He would never leave her. She would never leave him.

They were anchored together. They were survivors.

They came together in a conflagration of desire and burning need. Always it would be this way with them. Always the need, always the desire, always the passion, always the love.

They gave equally, received equally, partners in all things.

When they lay lethargic and replete in each other arms, they both knew they had found within each other the comfort of home at last.

EPILOGUE

From the Journal of Sir William Graves

My mother did more for me in death than she ever did for me life. I was fascinated that death had come to her so quickly and without blood. I also harbored the thought that had I known what to do, I could have saved her.

So I became fascinated with the workings of the human body. I wanted to understand everything about it. But more I wanted to ensure that no one would die unnecessarily, and so I became a physician. That role eventually led me to Winnie.

I took great pleasure in watching her blossom over the years. When I told her that Jack Dodger was in the process of building a hospital because of a debt he owed to me, she decided to use the funds she'd gathered for a hospital to build a sanctuary instead, someplace to shelter women who found themselves living in fear as she once had. And she work tirelessly to have the laws changed so women would no longer be deemed as property. She stood strong in her defense of women's rights. I, who had been a criminal as a child, never expected to marry a woman who would one day find herself thrown in jail because she stood firm in her convictions that women should have the same rights as men.

I was proud to have such a revolutionary at my side.

She blessed me with three sons and two daughters. They were sharp, strong of will, and determined to make their way in the world, and in doing so, they brought us great joy.

Whit eventually became known by his father's title and while most of the aristocracy called him Avendale, to his mother, he remained Whit. To her everlasting relief, he was a far better man than the one who sired him.

Neither Winnie nor I ever attended another séance, but sometimes in the late hours of the night we would talk about that evening, and Mrs. Ponsby's revelations. On occasion, I like to think that she possessed a true talent for communicating with the dead, that she contacted my mother, and that she did forgive me. But forgiveness is a gift of the kind, and my mother had no kindness in her. So then I doubt the veracity of the words. Not that I need my mother's forgiveness, for I have Winnie and she forgives all my sins.

Knowing that the dead always reveal their secrets, I sometimes think I should burn this journal, but my secret is a relatively harmless one. I had told Catherine that she caught me in a compromising position with Winnie because I was attempting to seduce her so she would keep me near and I could better protect our secrets. But the truth was I could no more resist Winnie than I could cease to breathe.

Which, by all accounts, made me the last among our group of scoundrels to be brought to his knees because of his love for a woman.

If you enjoyed Graves's and Winnie's
story, see where it all began!
Fall in love with the *New York Times* and *USA Today*
bestselling
Scoundrels of St. James series,
available now wherever books are sold.

THE SCOUNDRELS OF
ST. JAMES SERIES

IN BED WITH THE DEVIL

BETWEEN THE DEVIL AND DESIRE

SURRENDER TO THE DEVIL

MIDNIGHT PLEASURES WITH A SCOUNDREL

And keep reading for a sneak peek from

WHEN THE DUKE WAS WICKED,

on sale February 2014,
from *New York Times* bestselling author Lorraine Heath.

An Excerpt from

WHEN THE DUKE WAS WICKED

The garden path was lit by gas lamps, and yet the darkness still dominated. Grace walked slowly, cautiously, searching through the shadows for a familiar silhouette. She wondered what Lovingdon wished to discuss with her and why he had chosen this setting rather than the parlor. He was always welcome in their home. He was well aware of that fact, although she did have to admit that the clandestine meeting appealed to her, the thought of doing that which she shouldn't.

And why so late at night? What was so urgent that it couldn't wait until morning? She was not usually lacking in imagination, but she was quite stumped.

"Grace."

She swung around. In the darkest recesses of the rose garden, she thought she could make out the form of a man. Her heart was hammering so strongly that she feared it might crack a rib. "Lovingdon?"

She watched as the shadows separated and he strolled toward her. "I wasn't certain you would come."

"I'd never ignore a summons from you. What's this about? What's—"

His strong arms latched around her as he pulled her from the path, into a corner where light could not seep. Before she could scream or utter a word of protest, he latched his mouth onto hers with such swiftness that she was momentarily disoriented. His large hand was suddenly resting against her throat, tilting up her chin as he angled her head, all the while urging her lips to part. She acquiesced and his tongue swept forcefully through her mouth, as though aspects of it needed to be explored and conquered.

With a sigh and a soft moan, she sank against him. She had thought about kissing him for far too long to resist—and his skill made resistance unappealing. His other arm came around her back, pressed her nearer. As tall as she was, she supposed she shouldn't have been surprised by how well they fit together, thigh to thigh, hips to hips, chest to chest, and yet she was taken off guard by the intimacy, the heat radiating off him.

His roughened thumb stroked the sensitive flesh beneath her chin, near her ear. No gloves, just bare flesh to bare flesh. A slight alteration of position and his fingers were working her buttons. One loosened. Two. Three.

She knew she should pull back now, should insist that he stop, but when his warm, moist mouth trailed along her throat, she did little more than tip her head back to give him easier access. Another button granted freedom, and his tongue dipped into the hollow at her throat. Fire surged through her, nearly scorched her from the inside out. Desire rolled in ever increasing waves.

He groaned, low and deep, his fingers pressing more insistently into her back as though he wished for her to become part of him, as though he couldn't tolerate even a hairbreadth separating them.

He dragged his lips up her neck, behind her ear. Then he was outlining the shell of her ear with his tongue, only to cease those delicious attentions in order to nibble on her lobe. She was close to sinking to the ground, her knees growing weak, her entire body becoming lethargic.

"Do you understand now," he rasped, "how, when a man desires a woman, his kiss might very well ruin her reputation?"

He desired her. A sensation, rich, sweet, and decadent coursed through her. He desired her. The words echoed through her mind, wove through her heart.

"But he is not likely to stop here," he murmured.

He? Who the devil was he talking about?

"He will leave no button undone, no skin covered. He will remove your clothes, lay you down on the grass, and have his way with you. You will cry out with pleasure only to weep with despair because you're ruined. If you're discovered, you'll be forced to marry him. If not discovered—"

He gave her a tiny shake and she realized his fingers were digging into her shoulders, jerking her out of her lethargy. She opened her eyes, and though they were in darkness, she could still feel the intensity of his gaze.

"You play with fire when you go into gardens with gentlemen."

ABOUT THE AUTHOR

LORRAINE HEATH wrote her first story at seven, and it involved a fisherman who fell in love with a mermaid. She has since moved on to writing about sexy cowboys and dashing English lords (and sometimes, cleverly, in the same book!). *Publishers Weekly* says she is a "master of her craft." She is indeed, and along with being a *New York Times* and *USA Today* bestseller, has won the RITA Award, four *Romantic Times* Reviewer's Choice Awards, and a Career Achievement Award.

Visit www.AuthorTracker.com for exclusive information on your favorite HarperCollins authors.

Give in to your impulses . . .
Read on for a sneak peek at four brand-new
e-book original tales of romance
from Avon Books.
Available now wherever e-books are sold.

ALL I WANT FOR CHRISTMAS IS A COWBOY
By Emma Cane, Jennifer Ryan, and Katie Lane

SANTA, BRING MY BABY BACK
By Cheryl Harper

THE CHRISTMAS COOKIE CHRONICLES: GRACE
By Lori Wilde

DESPERATELY SEEKING FIREMAN
A BACHELOR FIREMEN NOVELLA
By Jennifer Bernard

ALL I WANT FOR CHRISTMAS IS A COWBOY

by *Emma Cane, Jennifer Ryan, and Katie Lane*

What's better than Christmas?
Christmas and Cowboys.

From Emma Cane, Jennifer Ryan, and Katie
Lane come three wildly romantic holiday
stories featuring snowstorms, proposals,
a sleigh ride ... and, yes, cowboys.

The Christmas Cabin by Emma Cane

Sandy and her five-year-old son, Nate, are Christmas tree–hunting when a snowstorm strikes and an old ranch hand points them to an abandoned cabin. Little does Sandy know, the hand sent cowboy Doug Thalberg to the same place. It's a Christmas all of Valentine Valley will remember.

Can't Wait by Jennifer Ryan

Before The Hunted Series began ...

Though she is the woman of his dreams, Caleb Bowden knows his best friend's sister, Summer Turner, is off limits. He won't cross that line, which means Summer will just have to take matters into her own hands if she wants her cowboy for Christmas.

Baby It's Cold Outside by Katie Lane

Alana Hale hits the internet dating jackpot when she finds Clint McCormick. He's sensitive and responsible—not to mention wealthy. When he invites her to spend the holidays on his family's ranch, she readily accepts. But on the way there, a blizzard strands her with a womanizing rodeo cowboy who could change everything . . .

An Excerpt from

SANTA, BRING MY BABY BACK
by Cheryl Harper

A bride abandoned at the altar . . . just in time for
Christmas? 'Tis the season for second chances at
Cheryl Harper's Elvis-themed Rock'n'Rolla Hotel.

There was something about Grace Andersen that made him want to help, even after decades of trying to guard his mother and her money against personalities and stories like hers.

He wouldn't mind being Grace Andersen's hero.

To avoid doing something stupid, Charlie turned to go but stopped when she added, "Oh, Charlie, could you do me a favor?"

She shuffled toward him, the rustle of the wedding dress sweeping the floor loud in the silence. "Could you unzip me? I thought I was going to dislocate a shoulder getting it zipped in the first place." She turned and bent her head so that all Charlie could see was the smooth, pale skin of her shoulders and the loose dark hairs that tickled her neck.

When he didn't move quickly enough, she turned her head to look at him over one perfect shoulder.

Remembering to breathe became a struggle again.

He forced himself to step closer. He grasped the zipper with one hand and slid the other under the fabric. The zipper made a quiet hiss as it slid down the curve of her back, every centimeter showing more beautiful skin.

And out of the blue he wondered if unzipping Grace Andersen would ever get old. Finished, he took two steps away to keep from smoothing his hands over her shoulders like he wanted, or tracing a finger down her spine just to see goose bumps.

She turned her head. "Thanks."

As he pulled the door closed behind him, Charlie tried to remember the last time he'd seen anyone as pretty as she was in real life. Never. But she wasn't his type. He preferred career women who wore glasses and looked like they could reel off stock prices or legal precedents. He liked women with sharp minds and sturdy savings. He'd had enough excitement growing up with Willodean McMinn Holloway Luttrell Jackson. Now all he wanted was a comfortable home, an easy, companionable, stable relationship, and maybe a baby to keep things interesting. Maybe.

Grace Andersen looked like . . . magic.

He propped his hands on his hips and shook his head as he looked out at the guitar-shaped pool that was covered for the season.

Magic? He hadn't been in the hotel for a full twenty-four hours and already his mind was going. Something about being that close to her had melted it. But Grace Andersen was just a woman. She'd been left at the altar but didn't seem too broken up about it. He hoped her new plan, whatever it was, included checking out of the hotel immediately. Beautiful Grace Andersen might have the ability to wreck his goals along with his logic if she stayed.

An Excerpt from

THE CHRISTMAS COOKIE CHRONICLES: GRACE

by Lori Wilde

(Originally appeared in the print anthology
The Christmas Cookie Collection)

New York Times bestselling author
Lori Wilde returns to Twilight, Texas, for
another delightful holiday installment of
her *Christmas Cookie Chronicles*. And this
time, a young couple are thrilled to expect
the greatest gift of all: a new baby!

The perfect Christmas starts with the perfect tree . . .

Flynn MacGregor Calloway put a palm to her aching back, wrapped her other arm around her pregnant belly, canted her head, and studied the spindly-branched, lopsided Scotch pine. After much wrestling and a few choice words, she'd managed to get it set up in a corner of the living room in the cottage she shared with her husband, Jesse.

She'd wanted to surprise him, so she'd waited until after the morning wedding of Jesse's father, Sheriff Hondo Crouch, and his bride, Patsy Cross, before she'd slipped down to the Christmas tree lot and, using Jesse's pickup truck, drove the tree home. Jesse had volunteered to drive the newlyweds to DFW airport to catch a plane bound for a Hawaii honeymoon, so he had taken their sedan because three people and luggage fit in it better, giving Flynn plenty of time to get it done.

The glow from the icicle lights dangling on the eaves outside slanted through the window and shone through some of the more meager limbs.

Okay, so it wasn't quite a Charlie Brown tree, but it was close and clearly not what Maven Styles, the author of *How to Host the Perfect Christmas*, had in mind when she declared that an impeccable holiday began with the perfect tree.

Then again, Maven Styles probably wasn't on a newlywed student's tight budget that required her to wait for Christmas Eve, when they marked down the trees. Flynn had picked this one up for five dollars, and she was proud of her bargain. Maybe not proud, but it was a real tree, not artificial, and seven feet tall. She should get points for that, right? All it needed were a few decorations to spiff it up.

She couldn't regret cutting corners. The baby had been a surprise, a very welcome surprise to be sure, but their finances had taken an added hit because of it. Between scraping together money for her college tuition, the cost of rebuilding Jesse's motorcycle shop after the fire, exorbitant health insurance for the self-employed, and getting ready for the baby's arrival, they hadn't much money left to spend on holiday celebrations. Their situation was a temporary setback, she knew that, but part of her couldn't help feeling wistful that their last Christmas with just the two of them was going to be as sparse as that scraggly Scotch pine.

Stop feeling sorry for yourself, she scolded. *Plenty of people have it much worse.*

By tightly pinching pennies all year and keeping an eagle eye out for sales, she'd managed to save just enough to buy Jesse a new leather jacket to replace the one he'd worn since high school. She couldn't wait to give it to him on Christmas morning. For now, it was wrapped and stowed in the trunk of their car. He'd had so little growing up that she ached to give him everything his heart desired. Which was why she'd checked *How to Host the Perfect Christmas* out of the library, hoping she could pick up a few pointers.

A cardboard box filled with decorations from her childhood sat on the floor. Flynn peeled back the tape and opened the flaps. Her mother had had the habit of either buying or making one special ornament to commemorate each Christmas.

As she removed them from the box, each decoration stirred a memory—the candy canes made out of bread dough and shellacked (crumbling a bit now with age) that she and her younger sister, Carrie, had helped their mother bake in 1992. The twin wooden toy soldiers her mother's best friend, Marva Bullock, had given her after the twins, Noah and Joel, were born; and the last ornament her mother had ever purchased, a delicate red glass ball inset with a tiny nativity scene.

Air stilled in her lungs. Although her family hadn't known it at the time, the red glass ball represented the last perfect Christmas before her mother had been diagnosed with amyotrophic lateral sclerosis.

Tears misted her eyes. *Oh, Mama. You'll never know your grandchildren.* With a knuckle, she wiped away the tears. Should she put the ornament on the tree? It would stir painful memories every time she looked at it. And yet the ornament was a shining reminder of that one perfect Christmas when her family was last together and whole.

An Excerpt from

DESPERATELY
SEEKING FIREMAN
A Bachelor Firemen Novella

by Jennifer Bernard

From *USA Today* bestseller Jennifer Bernard
comes the steamy story of a sexy bachelor fireman
and the woman who will turn his life around.

Wayside Chapel, San Gabriel, California

The groom's side of the aisle was packed with an astonishingly high number of gorgeous men. Nita Moreno, standing near Melissa McGuire—soon to be Melissa Brody—surveyed the pews with widening eyes. There was enough testosterone in the building to fuel a small nation's army. Enough handsome, manly faces to fill an issue of *Playgirl*. Enough brawny muscles to . . .

Oops. Busted. From across the aisle, two steps behind Captain Brody, a pair of amused, tiger-striped eyes met hers. An unusual mixture of gold and green, surrounded by thick black eyelashes, they would have made their owner look feminine if he weren't one solid hunk of hard-packed male. A smile twitched at the corner of his mouth. Even in this context—the so-called Bachelor Firemen crowding the wedding of their revered fire captain—he stood out. First there was that breath-taking physique. Then there was his face, a study in contrasts. His features were so strong they almost qualified as harsh. Firm jaw, uncompromising cheekbones. A man's man . . . until one looked into those golden eyes, or noticed that he possessed the most beautiful mouth Nita had ever seen on a man.

She narrowed her own eyes and met him look for look. Hey, she wasn't checking out the available men. She had one of her own. Very deliberately, she let her gaze roam to the bride's side of the aisle and settle on Bradford Maddox the Fourth. Hedge fund operator, family scion, possessor of a killer business instinct and an only-slightly-receding hairline, he was hers, and she could still scarcely believe it. Maybe soon she and Bradford would be making their way down an aisle like this. Out of unconscious habit, she took the inside of her cheek between her teeth and worried it at. She loved Bradford, and she knew he felt the same. He must.

Bradford, who seemed lost in thought, startled when he realized she was looking adoringly at him. He gave her a faint smile, then pressed his finger to his ear. Lovely. He wasn't lost in thought, he was listening to his Bluetooth. She sighed, telling herself to let it go. It came with the territory when you dated a hotshot financier. Of course he couldn't focus his *entire* attention on the wedding of two people he didn't even know.

The right side of her body felt suddenly warm, and she realized the man across the aisle was still watching her, as if she fascinated him.

Really? *She* fascinated *him*? That seemed unlikely. She

raised a questioning eyebrow at him. He smiled, the expression transforming his face from the inside out. Goodness, the man was gorgeous, in a totally different way from Bradford. Dark instead of blond, tough instead of charming. Virile and primitive, the kind of man who would toss you over his shoulder and have his way with you.

He jerked his chin at her, as if signaling her to meet him in the chancel.

She frowned at him, scolding. *Excuse me?* How inappropriate.

He did it again, more urgently this time.

What did the man want? She lifted her hands, palms up—a frustrated question—as he mouthed something to her.

"Bouquet."

Aw, crap.